Incident at the Medallion Club

Incident at the Medallion Club

A novel by

J. Hayes Hurley

ISBN 978-1-257-74288-2

Publisher: Croesus Books

To Will and Maureen

Cover Art by Douglas Leichter

Chapter One

My name is Stephen Lattimore. In June 2002, after waiting seventeen years for the opportunity, I finally moved into my great-grandfather's suite at the Medallion Club in New York City. The man who was living in it, and who had been living in it for a decade before I moved into the club proper in 1985, died in his bed. He was a mean old man who never gave me the time of day save to laugh at me when I told him I wanted that suite.

I was number three on the waiting list. The man who was number one found he could not afford the suite when it did come up; the man who was number two entered a hospice three days before his chance arrived. As for me, I had, and still have the money to live in this suite, and I have my health, too. I would not characterize myself as mean, though I must say that an excessive amount of money can make a man cautious, selective, and in my case, reclusive. I will not lunch with any club member who tells me he is on a waiting list for my suite.

A few words about the Lattimores are in order. We are a Virginia family. We began acquiring land back in Colonial days and my first American ancestor used to tell everyone that although it was the case that he and George Washington were both land surveyors, they really did not know one another that well. The story is true, but the intent was to lead people to believe that our family was being modest about its involvement with our nation's founding fathers. There are lots of pesky ethical issues like that attached to our family I readily admit, but more of that later.

After more than a century of land dealings, good and bad, the Lattimores finally produced a genuine tycoon, Ely Lattimore, my great-grandfather. Born in 1860, Ely sold all our land holdings and made a fortune in the horse stirrup industry. He was one of the five founders of the Medallion Club of New York City in 1920. Each of the founders had his own suite and all five are located on the nineteenth floor of the club. Great-grandfather never lived here; he died the same year the club opened.

My grandfather, Stephen, born in 1900, did move to New York, and resided in the club from 1925 until his death in 1950. He, too, waited for his father's suite to become vacant, but in vain; he had to content himself with living in ordinary rooms, changing them from time to time as I did in my early days. One could say that my great-grandfather and my grandfather set a family precedent: a working generation to be followed by a gentlemanly generation. My grandfather never held a job; my great-grandfather's money, all of it left to Grandfather, ran out the month he died.

Grandfather did sire a child, my father, Ely Lattimore, in 1937, following a brief liaison with an employee of the Medallion Club. (Another of those pesky ethical issues, I suppose.) The two married briefly, for the sake of the child, then divorced. My father was raised back in Virginia by his mother, the ex-Medallion Club employee, and, like our ancestors, he got back into land dealings. Grandfather left him nothing in his will; there was nothing to leave. Father built a moderately successful real estate business with the help of his wife, Shirley, my mother. I am their only child.

I was born in 1964. My father was determined that I would not idle my life away as had his father, so they sent me away to school with the promise that I would be joining the family business the day I graduated. I agreed.

When I left New Haven and got back to Virginia the real estate market was undergoing a downward turn and there really was no opportunity for me to start contributing. I ended up living at my parent's house until they were killed in a car crash in early August.

It was a mysterious accident to say the least. At three o'clock in the afternoon on a clear day with little traffic and no motivating explanation save their reaction to a shaky housing market, my parents climbed into the family Buick and my father steered it off a secondary road, onto a temporary levee, and into the waters of the James River below Claremont. When the bodies were fished out of the water they showed no signs of struggle. They had neither unlocked their doors nor unhooked their seat belts. The insurance company suspected a case of double suicide.

"Are you accusing my parents of an ethical breach?" I shouted out, over and over again, to anyone who would listen.

That was what the insurance company thought, though they had no proof. They paid up; I was sole beneficiary.

Immediately, I settled the mortgages on our house. Then I sold it along with the rest of my parent's real estate holdings. I was urged not to do this; in fact I was urged to seek therapy. I ignored all pleas, be they financial or emotional. I placed all the cash I got in a bank, the interest rate of which was next to nothing. Once these transactions were completed I moved into the Medallion Club and started living off my principal, figuring it would take me eight years to do so. This was in 1985.

Chapter Two

The first five years went smoothly. I wanted Great-grandfather's suite and put in for it, even though getting it would have destroyed my eight-year plan. As it was I lived in single rooms and changing them frequently. If there were renovations in progress on the floor I was living on I requested a room change to avoid the bustle. If I grew sick of looking into an alley, I requested a room overlooking the street. If someone, at some time, booked the room I was currently living in well in advance, I cheerfully moved to wherever management placed me. Occasionally the club was completely booked and I could not move at all. This was the case when the incident at the Medallion Club began to unfold.

It was 1990 and I was staying in room 806. The eighth floor was to my liking; the corridor was bright and cheery. I had a queen sized bed yet the window of my particular room looked out on a street where garbage was picked up on Saturday nights. I became irritated by the noise and decided to make another change. I picked up the phone in my room.

"I am sorry, Mr. Lattimore, there are no rooms open this week?" Judy explained in her most droning voice, Judy being an assistant manager down at the front desk. We had dated a couple of times the previous year and during this period Judy called me Stephen, but when nothing came of our affair, thanks only to me, as Judy had it, I went back to being Mr. Lattimore, or just "sir," while I continued to refer to her as "Judy, and not "Miss Knoffer."

"No problem, Judy, I'll wait. Just let me know when you can shift me."

"Some time next week, sir, I would guess."

I still considered Judy a possible lover; I had Grandfather's blood in me, after all, while Judy now thought of me only as a guest, at least officially. I suppose I should have refrained from telling her during our first date that I was in all likelihood going to go broke within four years. I did add that not doing anything about anything was what one was *supposed* to do when one was idle and rich. Judy failed to grasp this finer point; she insisted that the tragic death of my parents had addled my brain and that I should seek help and a job, too.

I hung up the telephone and went out into the hallway, meaning to go to lunch when my attention was drawn to a conversation between Adele, the ever-attentive chambermaid on my floor, and a guest in room 813. The door to 813 was open and Adele, standing in the doorway with her arms wrapped around a vacuum cleaner handle, was speaking to a man about ten years older than me. I had never actually seen this room, and so I paused in front of the open door pretending to tie a shoelace, having no other motive than to take a peek into a room that I might one day come to occupy. Adele happened to be explaining to the guest what Judy had just explained to me.

"They do got rooms with queen sized beds, sir, but all are filled for now. How long you staying?"

The man standing in the room was a tall, scrawny fellow with a shock of blond hair and a pair of deep set, flint-blue eyes that stared out at everyone he turned to in the most disconcerting manner. As well, he had a booming voice that set one's teeth on edge.

"Not sure. Not sure," he answered. "I was invited here to give a talk, one of those literary luncheon talks? I'm a poet and I've come into town some days early to meet with friends and such. Call it an extended Thanksgiving vacation. But I don't like this two bed set up at all."

I decided to intervene.

"Hi, Adele, what is happening?" I asked, addressing the maid instead of this stranger but really speaking to him. Adele and I got along tolerably well, even though she took it personally whenever I made a "complaint" about things like stained shower curtains or tiny window leaks. I explained to her that "complaint" was too strong a word for use in these contexts and that all I was asking for were reasonable adjustments. Adele never saw things this way. She was a fifty-year old woman with hair dyed light red; she had a pleasant face and a tolerable figure. She always did do what I asked of her, but was not above fixing me with her eyes, much, I regret to say, like a psychiatrist on the offensive against a psychopathic patient lest he take complete charge of his own treatment.

Anyway, there I was in the corridor being watched by two upsetting pairs of eyes.

"Mr. Lattimore, this gentleman. . . ."

Adele caught herself gossiping and her voice abruptly faded away. She was letting me know that this 813 business was none of my business. Regardless, the man in the room suddenly boomed out in a cheerful voice, one that belied his harsh facial expression:

"I was just telling this nice lady that I wanted to change rooms. But she said they have no vacancies through the weekend."

"What's the problem with this one?" I asked, falling into a loud tone of voice myself.

"Come in and see!" he suggested, adding a smile to his face, one that opened up his lips like a pair of cutting shears. Adele stayed where she was, as if symbolically blocking my entrance. I squeezed right by her and into the room. I liked the setup right away. I could see the place was relatively large and that it overlooked a quiet courtyard.

"Jeremy Lighter," the tall man said, offering me his hand to shake.

"Stephen Lattimore."

His handshake was firm and I returned a solid grip. Adele eyed the both of us now, ready to defend herself regarding the hands on maintenance of either room.

"The room is fine," I said, craning my neck towards the open bathroom door. "Why do you want to move, Jeremy?"

"I just don't like having two double beds is all."

I walked into the bathroom. Everything looked in order. Then, with a smile for Jeremy, I crossed in front of him and helped myself to a peek in the clothes closet.

"I tell you what," I said. "I like your room. I have a queen bed in mine. Come and see. If you like it we can switch."

"Great! Let's do it," Jeremy boomed. His hard blue eyes stared right through me even as his steel-bladed smile widened.

"You gotta ask the desk," Adele hastened to say. I did not at the time know what drove that woman. She did not trust me, or else she found me very attractive, for even back then I suspected the latter. I was a reasonably good looking young man and one of the advantages of living in the club is that I can engage in any number of casual affairs and on any social level I choose.

"Don't worry about it, Adele. I am just going to show him my room. If he likes it we will be sure to tell the desk."

I turned back to Jeremy and gestured broadly with my arm.

"Shall we? I am right down at the end of the hall.

We both squeezed past Adele, who stood holding onto her vacuum cleaner handle like a security guard holding a deadly weapon. We looked to the right and left as we headed toward my room, glancing at the framed pictures hanging on the walls. These were photographs of famous Medallion Club members dating back decades. I opened my own door and Jeremy went in to look, striding about much as I had in his room.

"Ah. Perfect. Perfect. Why don't we switch?"

At this juncture a twinge of guilt took me and I hastened to warn Jeremy of something.

"Hold it. Let me confess. The pipes sing when you shower."

I did not mention the Saturday night garbage collection.

Jeremy shot me his penetrating look and then he burst out laughing.

"I don't believe it, Stephen. I am talking to a man with scruples to bear, to a man that is willing to vocalize his guilt, and in this decadent age? Put yourself at ease, will you? I like looking out on the street. I like the bed and as for the pipes, good! I can make all the noise I want in the shower. What do you say? We do it?"

"We do it."

I got right on the telephone. While I was buzzing the desk Adele stuck her head in my door. Jeremy caught my eye and this time we both burst out laughing.

"Hi, Judy? This is Stephen. *Mr. Lattimore*. The fellow in 813? Yes. Jeremy Lighter. He wants to switch rooms with me. So why don't we just go ahead. What. Oh."

I looked up and said to Jeremy:

"She is seeing if anyone has booked this particular room in the weeks ahead. There is always the possibility that I will find myself out on the sidewalk now and again."

"You live here full time?" Jeremy asked, more than mildly surprised.

"Despite my age," I said, smiling. "Hello? Good! Well. Do we have to sign or something? OK. All right. Good."

I hung up and clapped my hands.

"It's all set. You can move your things in here and I can do the same with your room. We can exchange keys now. Judy, the desk girl, the assistant manager I should say, is punching the right buttons."

An uncanny feeling shot through me, that of unexpected elation, and I do believe that Jeremy Lighter felt the same thrill. There was no call for it, all we were doing was making a simple room exchange and yet there it was. Adele's face fell in turn. There was no call for her reaction, either.

For the next ten minutes Jeremy and I passed one another in the corridor while hauling our suitcases and miscellaneous items in opposite directions. It was only when we were finished and I returned to what was now his room 806 to say a quick thanks that it occurred to me to ask him:

"I overhead you say you're a poet, Jeremy?"

"I am afraid so."

"I guess I don't know of you."

Jeremy gave a sharp guffaw.

"Don't go apologizing for that, too, Stephen. Virtually no one in the world has heard of Jeremy Lighter."

"Some important folks must have; they invited you to speak at a literary affair here at he club, didn't they?"

"That is true. I do have a small but loyal literary following."

"I like poetry," I blurted out, which was a whopping white lie. In truth I had not gotten my eyes all the way through three serious poems in my entire life. I just felt that saying what I said to Jeremy was the appropriate, or decorative thing to say. Unfortunately, my mouth kept on running. "I would like to read . . . that is . . . can I get . . . ?"

Jeremy fixed his flint-blue eyes on me. I felt as if I was being X-rayed. I did not like that feeling. Then he said in a low, but still resonating voice:

"I have already left you a gift of my poems, Stephen. I left a volume of my earliest efforts on the dresser in 813. I do that to people, I will admit. It is my way of self-promoting. Leave people a book when you are leaving their presence and you can be both bold and shy at once. I do like being bold, by the way."

"Well, thank you. When is your talk? I haven't glanced at the calendar for this month."

"Not for another ten days."

"Well, welcome to New York, Jeremy Lighter, poet. Let's have lunch while you are here."

"That would be great. Give me a call soon. Or, I'll call you!"

We shook hands again and I made my exit. Adele walked me back to my new room.

"I gotta finish cleaning it, now, Mr. Lattimore."

"Give me a few minutes to sort out my clothes, Adele. Will you?"

"If you say."

I let my hand trail across her shoulder as I went on ahead and her eyes followed me into room 813 with what had to be a reciprocal touch. Still, when I closed the door behind me I felt as if I was escaping a bad situation. It was the oddest thing; ever since I had moved into this club Adele had taken it upon herself to assume any number of unspoken, incomplete, or merely suggestive roles in my life, roles that I reacted to in a consistently neutral manner. It was as if she would not let me play the bachelor unattended and utterly carefree, but wanted to introduce all sorts of lingering, trapped or childish considerations into my personal life. Who was this chambermaid, anyway, and who did she think she was pretending to be my mother, my lover, my keeper, my judge and my false accuser? Then again, I had no one to relate to on an ongoing basis and I rarely saw anyone whom I could consider an anchoring force. My so-called affairs, or tentative affairs with girls like Judy, proved to be of a very short duration at best and since I had no business to keep me occupied day in and day out save for my gentlemanly, late night writing, the silliest plots were hatched in my imagination alone and all of them, I suspected, could be easily triggered by the stern look of a maid, or by the critical tone of voice of a waiter, or by the momentary impatience of a concierge or by the kind look of a desk clerk or whomever.

I really did not care a whit about conjecture, yet these looks, these details, invariably plunged me into moods that I could not shake. The fact of the matter was that I had transferred all of the baggage of my childhood and of my young adulthood tragedy into this clubby setting here in Manhattan where it did not fit my status. If one had money one could adopt the right life style, one could live the right sort of life, if only for a few years. That I did. But no one can erase the silly moods that color our lives even as we live them properly.

I looked around again and nodded in satisfaction. I generally preferred rooms with double beds in them. I could lay clothes out on the unused bed. I could just jump up in the middle of the night and switch beds if I was having trouble sleeping. I could mess one bed up watching television or snacking, then sleep under clean sheets in the spare bed. I could have a guest stay over without having to call for an extra portable divan and I could always shove the two beds together if that guest happened to be a lady. I was already dressed to go out for lunch; I had on a blue oxford shirt, dress slacks and a cashmere sport coat, but I donned a light wool sweater as well, thinking there might be a chill in the air as it was well-along into fall. It was only then that I noticed the book lying on the dresser. It was a beat up volume and it bulged in the middle, perhaps from a lot of thumbing through or from water damage. I picked it up and read the title.

Guilt Takes a Holiday and Other Poems, by Jeremy Lighter. Turning the book over, I was greeted by a picture of a younger Jeremy, a man who was then about my age, standing on a street corner. He looked downright gaunt in this snapshot, which made him appear even taller than he was. It did not help that, in the picture, he wore his unruly hair down below his shoulders. It looked like a blond bush growing out of his head. The piercing blue eyes were the same, as was the scissors-like smile. The man was both likable and disturbing at once, even when reduced to the confines of a modest-sized book cover. I turned the inside cover and read his brief biography. Only one line caught my full attention.

"Mr. Lighter lives in Virginia, where he is a school teacher."

"Virginia!" I said aloud.

It wasn't much to go on, really. I supposed I would have to read his poems to get an idea of the man. This brought a smile to my lips.

"That is what the man had in mind for me, too."

Chapter Three

I carried the book in my hand and went down to the lobby. I meant to go straight from the elevator to the exit, ignoring Judy, but she called out to me.

"Mr. Lattimore!" Then more softly: "Stephen. It is all set. I switched you both."

I liked that conciliatory tone in her voice. I walked over to where she sat behind her counter.

"Hi, Judy. Thank you."

Judy was looking sexy despite being dressed in a somber, violet-colored business suit. Her dark brown hair was pulled tightly back from her smooth forehead and her cheekbones looked as if a practiced surgeon had artfully constructed them. In turn, her chin was small and her mouth was little more than a crimson stain. Upon the wide expanse of her forehead danced reflections from the muted lights of the club's marbled lobby. Judy would never pass muster on a model's ramp nor would she pass a screen test, but close up and in person she was astonishingly attractive and it excited me to look at her.

"It was nothing."

"Judy?"

"Yes?"

"Why don't we just get back together for Christ's sake?"

"I don't think so, Mr. Lattimore."

"Bother my last name. Will you think about it, at least?"

Judy's strong, Protestant, displaced mid-western work ethic suddenly took hold of her better judgment and this change became broadcast all over her top-heavy face for a moment.

"It is up to you, Stephen. You know what I mean."

"So it is. So it is."

What she really wanted to say was that if I were willing to get up off my ass, get a job and make something of myself, then she would be willing to date me again. I suppose that Judy, being an employee rather than a member of the Medallion club, saw nothing glamorous or adventuresome or mysterious or sophisticated about a man living alone in this place, scarcely interacting with the other club members and otherwise showing himself to be completely idle. She definitely did not see me as a romantic, much less as a tragic figure. The woman was sexy, yes, but she had no true sense of ambience. I gave her my best smile.

"Can you take a lunch break? I'm going to wander around in the city. I'll buy you something nice to eat."

"No thank you."

"Maybe another time then."

She did not answer. I gave a short wave good-bye, said hello to vacant-eyed Timothy, the young concierge-trainee on duty, and went outside. It was a chilly day after all and I was thankful for having added a sweater. I turned right on Forty-fourth Street and headed my steps west. The air was clear and the noonday sun was brilliant despite the cool temperature. I thought I would take my time looking about for a place to have lunch. Meandering was then and still is the sort of non-activity that filled my days. I could, and usually did agonize all morning long over where to have lunch, and then agonize well into the evening over where to have supper. More often than not I ate lunch at the Medallion Club, preferring the leather-lined, smoky billiards room. On that day I wanted to go outside. I came to this same crossroads often enough: should I stay inside the club with no idea what was happening in the city or the world at large, or should I go outside and wander the streets like one wandering the pathways of an amusement park?

This latter bit of description remains true up to a degree. New York is a great city if you have capital; all you have to do is meander around until you enter a place at will and without worry, knowing that you are keeping the metaphorical money-meter from ticking too loudly in your skull.

The idea of a meter ticking in one's skull was one I got from a classmate of mine who came to stay with me from time to time when I first moved into the club. This fellow, Josh Rider, was, back then, burdened by eighty thousand dollars worth of student loan obligations and since he could not find a job in Manhattan, a place where he longed to be, he was busy applying to law schools instead.

"The only way to avoid paying those loans is to borrow more money," he explained.

"You want to be a lawyer, Josh?"

He gave me a hurt-filled glance. Josh always had that "poor soul" look about him. His mouth was usually agape, his hair matted down on his scalp, and his eyes filled with imagined terrors. He was a short man, too; no doubt he felt as if the world was out to punish him for that and on top of all else. He said, once, wistfully:

"I want to set up a life for myself here in the big city, Stephen. I want to go to shows, to restaurants, to concerts, to art galleries, to museums, to gourmet shops, to boutiques, to openings and to parties. Yet I cannot rid myself of the sound of a meter, like that of a taximeter, ticking away inside me wherever I go. Even when you are at idle, the meter goes on ticking. A man could go mad worrying about the bill awaiting him."

Josh had a point but I did not take it; actually I muffled the sound. He did go to law school, by the way, and he got a job in a small Connecticut town doing corporate legal work on some sort of outside contractor basis. He called me up now and again. He began paying off his student loans as would a criminal his debt to society, working eighty hours a week at a job he hated and that came to one hour of labor for every thousand dollars of undergraduate educational loans, not counting what he borrowed to go to law school, while living in a drab condo up in Connecticut where he was altogether miserable knowing he had dug a hole for himself from which he would in all likelihood, or as far as I could calculate it, never climb out of in this lifetime. I kept inviting him to come to New York for another visit, but he kept turning me down.

"I haven't got the energy to come into the city any more," he explained to me once. "I am consumed."

I changed my mind about hours of wandering because of the chill and turned into the Algonquin for lunch. I liked what they had done with the Algonquin public rooms and I felt quite cozy sitting by myself in a small loveseat near the entrance to the famous bar. I thought about "poor soul" Josh, and I could not suppress a snorting laugh, for I had plenty of money in my pocket, at least for the short term. I did not even feel anxiety over my situation. Despite by upbringing I identified more with my grandfather than with my hard-working father. Idleness was all I really asked out of life and I got just that by walking about the city, by eating lunch and dinner, and by being conscientiously inactive save for my scribbling in the wee hours.

Josh's pent up desires were not my desires. In the five years I had been in New York I had not frantically dashed about attending shows, concerts, museums and the like; I had no desire to do so and I still have no desire to do so. Back then I did take my dates to some of these entertainment places at their express request, but more often than not I preferred to take them to restaurants where we could eat and converse for three hours at a stretch. While I am capable of understanding arguments I prefer to be phatically congenial. Stephen Lattimore, intrepid dining companion; that was I in a nutshell. The best of me is an easy picture to draw: imagine my elbows on the table, a pretty girl's elbows on the table, our foreheads almost touching, our hair tickling one another, our wine glasses being filled over and over again by whisper-quiet waiters and our having nothing to look forward to but dessert, after dinner drinks and maybe a bit of casual carnal pleasure. Broadway musicals gave me a headache, museums gave me sore feet, art openings left me grubbing for the cheese, and I would rather shop by concierge than to hang around boutiques feeling fabrics. To me, New York was the greatest city because one can go out and eat in quality places without count. That, and the comforts of the Medallion Club were all I asked from life no matter how short that life might prove to be.

"Damn."

I remembered, that moment, the book of poems I had lugged along with me by that loud-voiced fellow, Jeremy Lighter. I had no desire to read his work. Yet if he asked me to lunch, then . . . I sighed and opened the book of poems thrust upon me as a present.

When I did so there fell out onto the tablecloth a packet of some sort. Obviously that was what was making the volume bulge. It was an ordinary envelope, this packet. It was not sealed and the contents were already visible beside my wine glass. I was not being nosy; I merely looked down and saw what was there.

They were lottery tickets. There must have been a dozen of them. I shoved them back into the envelope, put this in the vest pocket of my sport coat, and made my way to the row of lobby telephone booths. I called the Medallion Club right away. Jeremy was in his room. His voice boomed over the phone lines.

"Oh, hello, Stephen. What's up?"

"Hi, Jeremy. I was just about to start reading your book when these lottery tickets fell out of it. I'll bring them back after lunch."

There was a longish pause and then he said:

"Hey! What can I tell you? Whenever I get into any big city I buy a bunch of quick picks. A waste of time, really."

"That is what I have found. I never buy them anymore myself."

"Tell you what. Are you in the club or in the city right now?"

"I'm in the city."

"I am soon off to meet with my fellow poets. I don't know when I'll be back. Would you do me a favor?"

"Shoot."

"Don't go out of your way or anything. But if you happen to pass a . . . I don't know . . . what do you call them, candy stores? Outlets? If you pass a lottery outlet would you check my quick picks for me? Come to think of it, I bought them in Grand Central when I first got here. I know you'll be wasting your time but just to confirm that I wasted my money it . . . will you do that?"

"Of course."

"Good. Thanks."

"No need to mention it."

"We won't mention it again, either one of us. And Stephen!"

"Yeah?"

"Lunch tomorrow?"

"Sounds good. You play pool?"

"I do."

"How about the billiards room at noon?"

"Like it. Bye."

I went back to nursing my second glass of wine. When I finished the wine I ordered a glass of single malt Scotch whiskey, neat, and by the time I left the Algonquin it was nearly three in the afternoon. I had entered the place around noon and so I considered lunch a success. I walked back to the Medallion Club, waved to Judy without going over to where she worked and took the curving marble stairs up to the main lounge. I sat in a leather chair and read the New York Times from cover to cover. I smoked a cigar, giving in to the fashion, and was preparing to return to my room for a nap when, to my irritation, I remembered I had promised to check those quick picks for Jeremy.

I was tired. I slept no more than four hours a night, holding to a strict rule, so I was used to taking a two to three hour siesta between lunch and supper. Caught in the grip of my habitual fatigue at this time of day I thought of just tossing the tickets. What the hell is the difference? I argued with myself. People have more chance of being drafted into the Presidency than they do winning the lottery. Nevertheless I got up and went outside again. I do not really know why.

I found the nearest lottery outlet in Grand Central Station and rather than having the harried clerk run twelve quick picks through the machine for me, I picked up a copy of the winning numbers and went on to the lobby of the Grand Hyatt where I plopped down in an easy chair on the mezzanine level. I actually nodded to sleep in my chair, for my delayed siesta was making an almost drug-like demand on me. Missing a nap, or even delaying a nap, could be hell. When I woke up again, only a half hour later, I felt out of sorts and cranky but I still had my duty to do. I ran though the pile of tickets, my voice humming along in a low undertone.

"Loser, loser, loser, loser, loser, loser, loser, loser, loser, loser, loser. . . ."

The blur of numbers on the control slip and on the last ticket in the bunch I held in my lap made a buzzing sound go off in my head of a sudden. I tried to look at those numbers again, on both bits of paper but I could not. I was suddenly covered in sweat as adrenaline shot through my body. Somehow I knew that those numbers matched. I knew that even if I was unable to see anything at the moment and had a headache and a pounding heart as well. Still, I had to be sure. So I took a deep breath, wiped my face with a napkin I found on the coffee table in front of me and forced myself to look at both sets of numbers, over and over, for a good thirty seconds. There could be no doubt about it. Jeremy Lighter, poet and fellow Virginian, was now worth thirty seven million dollars.

I put the winning ticket in my wallet. Then I got up and went over to the cocktail lounge in the mezzanine, inadvertently letting the other tickets fall on the floor as I went. I almost went back and picked up the losing tickets, meaning to discard them in a trash bin, but I did not; shock was interfering with the effectiveness of my millstone-like scruples.

I ordered a martini and sipped this for a good hour while waiting for my heartbeat to return to normal. Then I walked back to the Medallion Club with measured steps.

"What's up?" Judy called out. She was about to stop working for the day and her mood was rising. She had her coat on and her replacement was already seated.

"Everything," I said without stopping. Judy looked disappointed. I guess I was a bit rude but I did not feel like talking to anyone. I rode the elevator back to the eighth floor and went directly to Jeremy's room 806. I was going to knock but then I remembered that he was probably off with his poet friends and I stayed my hand. I went to my own room, took off my clothes, laid them out on the spare bed and climbed into the bed closest the window. I am a creature of habit and I had to have my full nap.

Chapter Four

My telephone rang just before noon.

"Stephen?"

Jeremy's booming voice sounded as familiar to me now as did my own.

"Yo."

"Going to lunch?"

"Of course. Join you in ten minutes."

I put on a pair of light wool slacks, a white shirt, a wide-striped silk tie and a double breasted blue blazer and took the elevator down to the billiards room. Jeremy was waiting for me in front of the projection T.V.

"Good day, Jeremy."

"And to you, Stephen. Where shall we sit?"

"I like this corner," I said, pointing to my right. We went over to where the smoke-stained, leather coatings reached all the way down to table level and took a table that was free. Jeremy looked around at the faded murals spread over this old leather and up at the groined ceiling, then he turned his sharp-eyed look upon me.

"What's the good word, Stephen? What's up?"

I managed to meet his glance head on and without blinking. "Nothing much, my friend. How did it go with your fellow poets?"

Jeremy let his look linger upon me for a moment too long, or so it seemed to me, and then carefully broke out his cutting tool smile. He displayed a kind of boyish enthusiasm that seemed at odds with his severe facial expression. Altogether he gave me the impression of being deeply involved in what people call the inner life, of being both tortured and uninhibited, passionate and blocked, at once. Perhaps he was bursting at the seams with this hidden tension and caught up in the quiet nobility of suffering as well. We were exact opposites I suspected, meaning that I would not trade places with him on a bet.

"It was great! There are six of us who belong to a single poetry reading group. We get together in the city twice a year and regale one another with our latest efforts. The nice thing about it is that we have unanimously agreed to ban any and all critical commentary. We just listen to one another recite, we always recite with unaffected rapture, and then we cheer like mad when a poem is so declaimed."

"I like that no critic rule."

"Yes and once the big poems are recited we take turns standing up, like men and women giving toasts, and we toss off single lines, or single stanzas with increasingly explosive results. And that doesn't even take our drinking into account. I tell you, Stephen, these gatherings fill us with ecstasy."

"It does sound wonderful for you."

"It is wonderful."

"I begin to understand how you feel, having glanced at your work," I lied. I had simply not gotten around to looking at his poems.

"Thank you, Stephen. It is comforting to know that someone has an inkling of what makes me tick."

"Oh I can't say I know you as yet," I said, trying to cover my tracks in case he asked me about any specific poem. "But I would like to learn. I would like to know about, ah, the motivation for your work."

I ordered a cheeseburger and Jeremy a club sandwich. We both called for bottles of Bass Ale. He went on talking about his poetry group and how much pleasure he got out of meeting with them. There was no doubt at all that the man was on fire with love for his writing art. He told me about his being selected to give a literary luncheon talk here at the club through the auspices of one of his publishers and how proud he was to accept the honor.

"Poetry is a whole, diamond-hard life within a life, Stephen. It pays next to nothing, if you are lucky. Mostly it is conducted like a relatively inexpensive hobby. No one pays us to travel from here to meet with one another or to recite before a group. No one gives us royalties we can live on. There are fewer and fewer grants we can apply for; I have given up that depressing process myself."

"What about your publications?"

"Our publications are lost leaders for publishers."

"So you have to work to live."

"Ah, yes. I am a teacher."

"Still, my friend, you are describing a busy and fulfilling life, are you not?"

Jeremy nodded his head without, for once, looking at me with those flint-blue eyes of his. I saw that I could draw this man out and he rushed on enthusiastically.

"I am, really. A poet's life is a life lived, as they used to say, on all eight cylinders; lines of poetry come to me even as I am busy fulfilling any number of routine responsibilities. I am always peering out at the surface in astonishment. I write poetry and I feel rich!"

"What do you teach?"

"Eighth grade math."

"You like it? You don't like it?"

"Those are not the right questions, Stephen. Not the right questions to ask a poet."

"Give me a clue, then. Give me answers to questions I am too dumb to ask."

"All right, then; think of me as being four people at once. I am the poet who writes particular works of art. I am the critic who evaluates these particular works of art. I am my own aesthetic theorist and, finally, I am the analyst who examines the very concepts that go into my own aesthetic theory."

"Wow. Do you, ah . . . count syllables or . . . ?"

"I am not talking about the technical considerations of language just here; rhyme and meter are a poet's nuts and bolts of course, but I am talking about . . . if you will permit . . . ways of seeing the world. I am driven by the contextualism of what I see, not so much by what I write. Of course I do get into questions of meaning, of sensual rendering, of structure, of distance, isolationism, dispassionate viewing, form versus expression and . . . but again those are technical considerations."

As he spoke to me his shock of yellow hair appeared electrified, his flint-blue eyes showed rage and his scissors-like lips warned of violence. I could not help but wonder; does he present himself this way to everyone on the earth, friend or foe, acquaintance or stranger alike, or was Jeremy Lighter targeting me, alone, because he thought I was hiding something from him? I figured I would eventually find out the answer to that question the way a poker player finds out what is in an opponent's hand at the showdown

The food arrived and we said little while we ate and drank. It was delightful.

"Another ale, Jeremy?" I asked, pulling the signing card to myself to indicate that the lunch was on me.

"Of course. Why don't we play some pool as well?"

I don't think Jeremy was a man interested in the niceties of pool playing, but I do think he needed to be roaming about just a little if he was going to continue speaking seriously to me. As for myself, I was taking a wait and see approach. My wallet was sitting in my breast pocket between my heart and the world. Now and again I patted at it from the outside of my blazer. We took our second round of drinks with us and selected our cues.

"You break," Jeremy commanded.

For some minutes we played nine-ball as earnestly as we had attacked our lunches. The only sounds to be heard were the clicking of the balls and the dry crunch of blue chalk on felt tips. At last Jeremy's face frightened me; I imagined, when he put the bottle of ale to his lips, that he would crush the brown glass in his cutting shear lips. I thought his flint-blue gaze would break the green felt liner on the pool table and I imagined that his breath could set the whole club on fire. Finally I asked him, with a studied casualness:

"Let's have it, my friend. Tell me a little about your theory of poetry. Or is it your theory of aesthetics?"

Jeremy looked down, making an obviously modest gesture with his free hand, then actually giggled for a moment.

"Perhaps I was bragging a bit. After all, my idea of poetry is individually tailored to my own use."

"Jeremy . . . you are a success! Now tell me, what was it that triggered your aesthetic awakening in the first place? What got you into writing poetry as a child?"

At once the giggle was gone and the terrible, blue-eyed stare was back. Jeremy looked at me from across the wide stretch of felt and said, with a sharp hiss:

"Theft!"

That buzzing sound, the one that went off in my head when I first realized there was an exact match between the control and the lottery ticket, was back torturing me again. This time I did not break out into a sweat and I did not swoon with fatigue. Instead, I presented Jeremy with my most innocuous smile, one that was not so much charming as it was disarming, and I worked my face up into the most amused and curious look that I could muster, saying, as sincere-sounding as I could muster:

"I want to hear about this."

Jeremy closed his eyes a moment, as if reaching down into his passionate poetic well. I found this encouraging. So long as he was busy exposing his own fiery soul there was less danger of his uncovering the secrets of my cooler psyche. He began to speak. As he did so we continued to play our games of pool and sip our bottles of ale, keeping a certain physical distance from one another the while.

One thing I counted on for sure: if Jeremy were suddenly to drop this pretext and call loudly for his winning lottery ticket, I would simply hand it over to him saying that I had been waiting for the right moment. I meant that. It was just that the right moment kept moving ahead of my present self as did my shadow my body.

"You were right to ask about a poet's childhood," he began. "The whole of one's aesthetic theory is usually formed in childhood. In my case it was a matter of deliberately substituting aesthetic values for ethical ones."

"Ethical?" I asked, blushing a bit. Jeremy did not notice.

"Oh, not quite like Baudelaire, of course. More like . . . well . . . Augustine."

He actually blushed a bit when he mentioned this name and this helped mask my own heightened color. I hastened to make him feel comfortable.

"It is all right. Just speak."

"I think I was . . . I don't know . . . six? I was all alone and playing under a catalpa tree in my back yard. It was June and the large leaves of this catalpa were newly green. It was just after the exotic blizzard of those white buds off their twigs and into the anchorless air. It was a time of light and shadow, one that revealed to me both the light green underneath and the dark green overlay of the leaves, of the filtering effect of sun through branches, of green and white, and black and gray, and of the hard yellow fire that hurt my eyes. I suppose my yard was a kind of Eden for a boy, one in which I could play in, and in all innocence. I had everything I wanted in this Eden, yet I was aware of something missing. I was aware of something . . . extraneous. Something that existed outside of my own realm of happiness."

"And what was that?"

"Toys. I . . . the neighbor boy next door to me had a great many toys. I thought he was rich because he had so many toys."

"I see."

"I said I was aware of this but of course I . . . I wasn't thinking about those toys, really. I was consciously happy while playing under the tree. But then, all at once, I experienced what I can only describe as a 'dark at day.'"

"In the Biblical sense?"

"No. I don't think it was quite like that. Let me tell you about it. I was alone in the yard and I happened to walk out from under the light and shadow effect created by the catalpa tree leaves and into the direct sunlight. There was this pure, harsh light shining down on me; I was literally bathed in it. That was the case. Then all of a sudden, and without my losing consciousness, sounds went away. I saw cars passing by on the street but they made no noise. I saw birds move their beaks but in silence. I accepted this at once. I accepted what came next as well. There came darkness. It was dark under the blazing sun."

"I don't follow you."

"I am telling you that I was both standing under the harsh yellow sun light *and* I was standing in an enveloping, muted darkness."

"What did you do?"

"I began to see myself, not from the outside, but from the inside, taking steps, leaving this Eden and going over to where the neighbor boy lived."

"How could you see yourself from 'inside'?"

"*I* was not the one who was willing this journey; I was the one being carried along in total innocence."

"And the dark at day?"

"The dark at day continued under the harsh light of the sun."

"So you entered the neighbor boy's yard."

"Right."

"And you stole one of his toys."

"I did. I took it back to my yard, back to Eden."

"Did you play with it?"

"No. That was the thing. I took it home with me and stuck it under the house. I stuck it in that fetid place between earth and wood and, for all I know, it is still there. Meantime, the darkness continued in the sun-lit world."

"Obviously, Jeremy, you were feeling guilty for having stolen that toy. Temptation caused you to see the world and to hear the world through dimmed senses. It is probably something that happens to a lot of people when they first 'sin' during childhood. It was a common psychological reaction I would say."

"Oh, I know that all right!" he boomed out. "I had stolen a toy and I felt guilty. But what attracted me was not the deed and not the guilt, but the dark! Do you see?"

"I am not sure I do."

"Before I committed *any* bad deed and before I felt *any* guilt there was the dark. There was the dark at day."

"I said that is what they call the temptation state."

"I don't know about that. Why can't the reduction just happen? In any case, forget about temptation! Forget about sinning and about guilt. I tell you . . . there was something *beautiful* about the dark at day. It was beautiful and it thrust all other considerations aside."

"If you don't consider this state you were in a kind of psychological mood, Jeremy, then what do you call it?"

"I think I experienced true privation."

"Privation of what?"

"Of spiritual reality."

"I see. That is why you mentioned Augustine. He stole pears; you stole an earthly toy and reduced yourself to standing outside what? Spiritual is too much of a word for me. I would say . . . what? The intellectual, or the metaphysical light instead?"

"Yes. Except that, for me, it was not so much a state that I wanted to flee as it was a state I found utterly fascinating."

"Fascinating?"

"I experienced privation of light *in* the sunlight and prior to my body's taking the toy. That was precious."

"I am trying to see this though your eyes, Jeremy but you do not make it easy for me."

"Imagine this. There is not one light here, the physical light, and another light there, the spiritual light; rather, there is the spiritual light, the physical light, at once, and then the spiritual light is gone."

"I am still trying."

"Before the dark at day I was bathed in two light sources. All of a sudden I was only bathed in one of them."

"How long did you remain in this state of privation?"

"Not very long at all. When I got over what I *did*, I was at once returned to the full benefit of both sources."

"You based your aesthetic theory on that?"

Jeremy did not say anything for a while. We ordered more ale and we pushed pool balls around with our cues and the poet seemed to be struggling with something altogether removed from this childhood tale he had told me. Finally he answered my question.

"Not exactly. The dark at day was beautiful, but it was not the source of my aesthetic theory in and of itself. It was not separate from it, either. It was . . . you see, Stephen . . . it was not this appreciation of the *less* that instructed me, ultimately, it was the experience of the *more!*"

"Less? More? I am afraid these metaphors escape me, Jeremy."

Jeremy eyed me suspiciously again and I was reminded of Adele's clutching her vacuum cleaner handle like a weapon and, quite involuntarily, my fists closed down hard upon my pool cue. I had no idea what this man would say next and I suppose I was preparing for the worst. Jeremy struggled for the right words as if fighting for air, and then he began speaking in a rush.

"When the spiritual light was returned to me along with the material light that never did flee, I understood that I had more, because I could now consciously see myself bathed in two lights at once, but without a logical operator separating them."

"I'll take your word for it."

"It is not that hard to grasp, Stephen. Once I was back being bathed in two light sources again, both the spiritual *and* the sensual light that never stopped pouring into my fleshy eyes, I had learned, by experience, not only to appreciate this life I was living, but to actually see more while living it. I began to see as a poet. I could see more as the poet who wrote the poems, while what I actually wrote about, in my poems, was the perverse beauty of the less! I had converted sin to beauty."

The ale we were drinking was making me logy. Suddenly I felt like arguing with Jeremy; suddenly I didn't care if he was an invited poet at my club. This whole business was weighing on me.

"Say that I grasp your theory as a theory of seeing. I am only 'seeing' your theory . . . to press the big metaphor, here . . . while you are claiming to see *reality* itself in a new way. There is a big difference here, is there not? I suppose that is why you are a poet and I am not. But tell me if I am grasping this in the wrong way: you claim that you actually see two light sources at once and without having to add a conjunction of this light and that light, right?"

"Right."

"But you mentioned setting aside the linguistic nuts and bolts of poetry before. The meter and rhyme and . . . I should think, Jeremy, that the words of the language stand in for what we *understand,* intellectually or spiritually or metaphysically, not for what we literally see. If you are claiming that you literally see intellectual light and have done so from childhood, then, well, your poems are merely the instances of reporting these sightings. Am I off base, here?"

"I say you are, Stephen. You have read my work. Surely you can see that I have both linguistic skills and intuitive insight."

He said this in a petulant tone of voice. I reminded myself that I was supposed to be careful, hoping he would not ask me something specific about one particular poem or other. I should have at least looked at the damn things I chided myself. Yet I could not resist sparring with him.

"What I mean is . . . how can you separate this ontological seeing, this gift that you have and with which you enhance your words on paper, from what ordinary people like me call the employment of meaning contexts?"

"My poems are not to do with meaning contexts. Not directly. They are descriptions of essence, fact, at once."

"Descriptions and not mere reporting? Where does all this seeing emanate from? What I am asking you is this: does your gift of seeing come from God, or from your own ego? What you describe is a gift, after all, and not a theory. Surely you can drop that pretense now."

Jeremy's blue eyes were smoking with what I took to be rage. I did not care. I was sure he was a fine poet: I gave him the benefit of the doubt. Still, I was not ready to grant him the further gifts of critic, theorist and analyst.

"The theory unfolds in the writing of the poems!" he thundered. 'The aesthetic seeing is a two-fold experience that I draw from . . . there is a difference. I . . . I . . . I lose the world of the really real during the dark at day and I recapture it upon its return. I then have restored to me the entire Umwelt!"

"The what?"

"The atmosphere! The environment! The Lifeworld! Where we all dwell in common!"

"The ambience of existence?"

"Call it what you like! It can be lived in the flesh alone, or with the mind or the soul properly engaged."

The man was getting angrier by the moment and so I hastened to say:

"I do begin to follow you now, Jeremy. You see what you write about; you write about what you see. Your readers, however, cannot see the light, literally, just by reading your words and understanding them, can they?"

"Can you?"

"Not yet, Jeremy. Not yet. But I wonder if . . . if I feel happiness, does this mean I know the essence of happiness? And if it does, does this mean we can substitute 'seeing' for knowing? While we are at it, why not use 'grasping' instead of seeing? It strikes me that some very fundamental philosophical mistakes are being made here. Of course, poetic license and all. I . . . I'm sorry. Do these questions help us at all?"

The man retreated into a sullen state and returned his pool cue to the rack. I returned my cue as well. I handed in my signed card for the lunch and was prepared to go on loitering in the billiards area until Jeremy made his exit but he seemed to recover all at once.

"I have another book of poems for you to read, Stephen. I think it will help dispel some of the difficulties we are having trying to communicate with one another."

"Oh. Good. How many volumes of poems have you actually published, by the way?"

"Four. Well, three are published and the fourth is just about to come out."

"That is a lot of volumes for such a relatively young man as you."

"I started young."

"So you did."

"Right after the dark at day."

"Of course."

I was tired now, dead tired. I was a creature of habit. I only wanted to go to my room and have a nap.

"I could give you that second volume now, if you like, Stephen."

"With or without another thirty seven million dollars hidden inside it?" I was tempted to say aloud.

"Sure. I'm heading back to the eighth floor anyway. We could do the book thing."

On the way up in the elevator and as we walked down the hall to room 806, any number of thoughts flashed in my mind. Jeremy Lighter could be a genius, a madman, a charlatan, a saint, a visionary, a repressed child, an artistic soul, a nervous wreck, a fascinating character, a dismissible oddball, or some such combination of all of the above. He certainly was high strung.

Adele was cleaning his room when we got to it. She wore her uniform with a few buttons open down the front, exposing her cleavage, and she stared at the both of us coming in together with her usual display of unease and sensuality, yet she made no move to leave the room once we were inside it. We ended up standing still while she worked around us. Finally I said:

"Adele? Would you give us a couple of minutes?"

"But I am cleaning, Mr. Lattimore."

"Adele?"

This served to bring her to an awareness of the situation and she left at once, but not before stopping at my side to say, in a near whisper:

"I got you some extra thick towels today. You will see."

"Thank you," I answered back in a whisper, lending a conspiratorial tone to our as yet unrealized relationship. Jeremy followed her out with amusement filling his flint-blue eyes. I wondered how humor could survive in those terrible orbs.

"The woman likes you, Stephen."

"Do you think so?"

"Of course."

We didn't talk about Adele any more. My mind raced, I was trying to think of something to say that would flatter Jeremy, for I was no longer entertaining the thought that he had recovered his bonhomie. I decided that I had hurt him and I knew I had done so without ever having looked at a single one of his poems. Once more, I was convinced that even if I did read those poems, the ones I had and the ones I was about to get, the situation would not change between us. I wasn't buying ontological seeing on top of the use of words as poetic description, but then again . . .

"I am thinking, Jeremy," I said aloud.

"Of what?"

"Oh, of . . . ah . . . a painter."

"Which painter?"

"Magritte."

He looked at me, carefully, and then ran his hand through his shaggy hair. He seemed to be calculating something. Finally he said:

"That is not bad. Magritte's painted images are there to be compared to my written images; is that what you are trying to tell me? That I construct bizarre mental images that are supposed to float in the air before the eyes of all mankind?"

"I am only throwing out a name, Jeremy."

"But with painters, of any sort, the question always remains: Do they paint what they see, or do they put images down on canvas according to the particular dictates of their talent, those talents being conveyed from brain to hand and then sent on from hand to brush, so that it is only afterwards they get around to inventing their insights or their visions through language? I am not sure about painting. Painting is not poetry."

"Sometimes it is useful to make comparisons."

There could be no doubt about the fact that Jeremy Lighter and I were at odds with one another. The question was, at odds over what? In a way I was horrified; in a way thrilled.

He was breathing very slowly now and I wanted very much to get out of his room. He seemed to forget I was there for a moment or two but then he stepped quickly to his bureau and opened one of the drawers. He pulled out a large leather satchel, opened this, and extracted another book. It looked much the same as the first book, it was slim and with a white cover. The only difference was that this one did not bulge in the middle.

"Here."

I took it into my hands and read aloud:

"Shame and the Other, by Jeremy Lighter."

"I suppose I follow a distinct pattern," Jeremy said with a wry but still cutting smile.

"Shame comes after guilt?"

Jeremy did not answer me. Instead, he went rummaging in his large satchel once again. He sat down on the edge of his bed and stuck both hands inside it. I thought he was looking for a third volume of poems, for ammunition that would serve as answer to my questions, but what he pulled out of that bag was something altogether different.

"Look at this, Stephen."

"Good God!"

What he held in his hand was a nasty looking revolver. I knew nothing about guns but this one struck me as being very thick and very smooth all at once. I never imagined these pistols could have such a thickness to them.

"It is a forty five caliber. What do you think of it? Here, get a feel of it."

"No thanks," I said, backing away from it as he offered it to me. "It looks like it could tear me in half."

"It could at that."

There were lots of things I did not want to think about at that moment, so I hastened to say:

"Jeremy? What are you, a poet, doing with a fat hand gun like that?"

He only laughed. His laugh sounded particularly ugly in my ears.

"I said that my life, as a poet, is enveloped in my life at large. This gun is part of the larger focus."

"Like teaching eighth grade math?"

Jeremy looked at me and his metal-lipped smile seemed especially cruel.

"Read the poems in the second volume, Stephen. As a favor to me."

I left him there holding onto that thick, bulbous revolver and made my exit. I backed out of the room as I went; I thought, irrationally, that the lottery ticket in my breast pocket would save me if it caught a forty five-caliber bullet before that missile slammed into my protective body. More crazy thoughts like that ran through my head as I finally made it all the way to my own room. I suppose I should have had a good talk with myself but I did not, I gave myself up to my nap. I am a creature of habit first and foremost.

Chapter Five

Josh Rider surprised me with a phone call on the following day. "Stephen! What are you doing?"

I recognized who he was, yet his voice seemed so different over the telephone. He sounded upbeat and confident. This was not the "poor soul" Josh Rider I had come to be so fond of since our undergraduate days.

"I am not doing anything, Josh. How are you? *Where* are you?"

"I'm at the Mark. How about we have dinner together?"

"All right. Come on over here about eight, ah, I'll see if I can get us a reservation for the rooftop dining room."

"No, no! You get over here to the Mark. I want to treat you."

"Josh? Are you sure you can afford this?"

"Don't worry, Stephen, it is covered."

"If you say so. The lobby at eight?"

"Great!"

When I arrived in the lobby of the Mark I did not immediately recognize the young man who came forward to shake my hand. Josh was actually looking good, for him. His mouth, which I would swear he had left hanging open from childhood, through his college days and on into the misery of his young adulthood, was now firmly closed and his jaw muscles, when he did exercise them into a broad smile directed at me, managed to keep the jawbone up so that he kept his two rows of teeth together. His hair, rather than being matted down, was fashionably cut and he wore an all too familiar three-piece suit of the sort I saw everyday at the club. Strange to say that although Josh appeared self-confident and utterly self-assured, he did not look either as endearing or as amusing to me as he did when his mouth was agape, his hair was a mess and he presented himself as a bona fide member of the "poor souls" club of the world.

"I am so happy to see you, Josh? What's up?"

"I'm in love, for one, Stephen."

"Love! Well. Tell me about it."

"I will. Let's have a drink before dinner. Come on."

This time it was Josh taking me by the elbow and guiding me through open foyer space and to the bar. This time it was Josh who patted me on the knee to let me know that this was his treat as he signaled the bartender. We ordered martinis and Josh began speaking in a rush.

"Her name is Jane and she is a fellow attorney."

"How romantic."

Josh ignored my throw away cynicism and once again I noted, sadly, that there had come about a complete change in my friend's character.

"I thought you were contracting for a big firm and not even showing your face in public, Josh. What happened?"

"All that is over, Stephen. I've been taken into The Hartford as an on-line corporate attorney. That's where I met my fiancée."

"Oh. I'm sorry for you. You always said that . . ."

"Sorry? Stephen? I am happy. I am in love, I'm getting married and all is well!"

"I see. I just thought that . . . well . . . you said you wanted to be in New York and delve into its endless offers of culture and that small towns drove you to despair and so forth."

"Forget about all that. I will get into New York often enough now, but not to live here. We are going to live outside Hartford."

"Small town again?"

"Yes. We're buying a house. Jane and I agree on just about everything."

So Jane and Josh were going to buy a house outside Hartford and work for a large corporation. It sounded perfectly boring to me. I gave him my best smile. Then I adopted a quizzical look.

"I thought you were buried, forever, beneath crippling student loan debt."

Josh was busy with the waiter who was bringing us our drinks for a moment but when he was free to answer my question he began nodding his head vigorously, as if telling me that he could solve a bad situation simply by agreeing to it.

"I have learned a lot about debt and debt management in the past year or so, Stephen. Really, it is all for the best. We are all on the same page in this society, or we ought to be; I have come to understand this at last."

"I guess I do not follow you."

"I am trying to tell you, Stephen, that I am over my immature whining stage. I am over the pursuit of my silly, undergraduate dreams as well."

"And your loans?"

"My total indebtedness through law school comes to one-hundred and twenty thousand dollars exclusive of any interest I'd have to pay. Jane's debts, which she had already begun to pay back with the interest folded in, come to around one hundred thousand dollars. That totals two hundred and twenty thousand dollars. I am going to start off, as a corporate attorney possessed of special skills I acquired while out on my own as a contractor, at a salary of one hundred thousand dollars yearly. If I produce, I will make considerably more money. Jane's present salary is one hundred and twenty thousand dollars a year and that will go sky high so long as she produces as she does. Jane plans to work full time for another five years or so and then to take time off so we can raise a family. She might go on half time or she might just quit for a period of years. It will be her decision. I am not pushing her in one way or the other. Jane is a traditionalist; I make no comment. In any case, we are looking good financially."

"And the house?"

"Closing next week. We bought in a new sub-division in West Simsbury, right outside Hartford? I figure that, in rush hour, we have about a thirty-minute commute, each way at most. That is damn good, Stephen."

"Must cost a lot to live out there."

"It does. But rates are good now. We got a mortgage of five hundred thousand at a sweet, six and one half percent rate. Jane had about one hundred thousand in stocks which we cashed in for the down payment on the dwelling and . . . this is the best part . . . we were able to fold our student loans into the obtained mortgage and so we save ourselves a three and a half percent differential on interest. Plus, we can pay both the house and the loans off over thirty years instead of worrying about ten year loans that would have buried us before we started. The house is worth six hundred thousand and assuming Jane and I both get raises of five percent per annum, and not even counting the merit bonuses and merit raises you get at the level we are at already, we should be able to make our payments and begin saving for retirement while standing on our ears. In fact, we are going to lease two BMW's next week. How does that sound?"

"It makes my head swim."

Josh laughed. We picked up our drinks and we toasted Jane in absentia.

"Where is Jane, by the way?"

"Jane's in Seattle this week at a conference on Lease and Buy Back Law. She is trying to get certain legislation changed for the benefit of the corporation. I've been sent here for a conference on Tax Credits. Details, Stephen! It's all in the details."

"You get a nice per diem, I see."

"Oh, that. You know, I have been out on the road three times in my first six weeks with The Hartford? You have to pace yourself. I learned that right away. I skip the big breakfasts and the lunches. I go to the meetings and only go to dinner with people who can be of use to me."

"Oh?"

Josh laughed. It was not a sound that was welcome to my ears. He sat across from me, small-boned, and rounded away in his new vest and coat jacket, looking for all the world like a young tom turkey. I suddenly expected him to lean over once again and rap me on the knee for reassurance and damn it if he did not do just that!

"This is down time, Stephen. I want to see you, man. What are you up to? Really. Any changes in your life?"

"No. I adhere to the same old schedule as always."

"You have a schedule? Really?"

"I do. I attend to my scribbling between the hours of midnight and six a.m., seven days a week."

"Writing? What do you write?"

"Oh, this and that."

"Where do you write?"

"I write at the desk in my room at the club."

Josh tried not to laugh at me but he did; a kind of popping snort came out of his pug nose. Then he tried to recover with a display of unpolished, even naked patronization.

"Same old Stephen Lattimore I knew in college. Chasing what are not so much impossible ideals as much as they are idiosyncratic ideals. You were always a peculiar chap. Come on, don't demure. *What* are you writing?"

I looked at my friend and made the conscious decision to retain my smile. He was going to laugh at me; guys like Josh always laughed.

"I will tell you what I am preparing, Josh, if you wish to hear it, even though I fear you will find my interests to be, ah, not only idiosyncratic, but grandiose as well."

"Oh, go ahead and tell me, Stephen. I can take it."

"I am writing a book outlining the proper life style of a gentleman of leisure. It is inspired by some notes my grandfather left in his Medallion Club room when he died."

Josh looked at me and, this time, his mouth did fall open. He actually *forgot* to laugh at me. I note this because Josh's laughing at *me* instead of vice versa was going to become our way of relating starting then and there with a drink at the Mark lounge. Finally Josh recovered his jaw muscles and his tongue and asked:

"Are you kidding?"

"No."

"Yes, but . . . Stephen? You can't sell a book like that. Can you? Who are you planning to sell this book to? How is it to be marketed?"

"Those questions do not concern me. I enjoy the way I live and I believe that what I do is representative of what ought to be the ultimate goal of all mankind."

"All mankind?"

Josh checked himself of a sudden, showing no further reaction to this latest gambit of mine. Then he looked furtively at his watch. I suppose he was thinking of inventing a business meeting that would irrevocably cancel our dinner. Still, he felt he had to ask me:

"Stephen? Jane and I are about to embark on life's greatest adventure. We have many struggles to face. Are you saying that what *you* do by yourself is better than what we are going to face as a couple?"

Funny how insults go; they mostly come along with the help people think they are offering you. I leaned over and tapped Josh on his knee this time. Then I looked him straight in the eye and said:

"Life's desperate *struggle* reminds me of so many moths beating their wings against a light globe without ever knowing that there are no answers in store for them should they succeed in breaking the glass. In a sense the true, inner light resides with idlers like me."

Josh sat back in recoil. He was no doubt making the mistake of thinking that I had just said something that was essentially insulting instead of essentially true. Jeremy might understand me. At least that tortured poet realized that our external deeds are merely there to be witnessed and that they do not count at all beyond some very shallow level of existence.

Josh recovered from my assault soon enough and when he resumed speaking to me again it was with a sly look in his eye.

"Could you give me an example, Stephen, of what ought to concern a gentleman of leisure? I must confess that the idea of leisure has been ripped from my personal lexicon. Jane and I give it all up for The Hartford day in and day out."

"My interests are quite eclectic, I'm afraid."

"Oh, Stephen. Just give me a sample. I told you what I am doing. Jane and I are trying to move tax credit legislation over to where it favors big corporations. What are you doing . . . from midnight till six a.m.?"

He said this last bit just to let me know that six hours work a day was hardly enough to justify one's overall existence and that doing so when most people were asleep did not change his opinion on the matter. I rode above this perceived barb.

"Of late I have been considering a group of theses once put forth by the Marquis de Condorcet."

"Who?"

He asked this while snorting through his little nose like a punk kid. He looked at me out of the corner of his eyes, and then daubed his nose with his napkin. He was clearly embarrassed for me. I just droned on:

"The only philosopher to take part in the French Revolution? Of particular interest to me is his conviction that the tyranny of the few over the many is perpetrated by an educated elite and that as a result of this the many suffer from what he called 'popular prejudice' precisely because they are kept in ignorance by those who are educated."

Josh looked at me that moment as he would a creature just in from outer space. Then he said:

"And?"

"I am not sure I agree with the Marquis."

Josh continued to fix me with an amused look, leaned an elbow on the table, raised one eyebrow and said, dragging out his words:

"Oh? Why not?"

"In the first place, lopping off a few heads in order to correct a factual, historical situation just will not suffice if what one seeks is real social change. There is nothing of either factual or historical significance connected with mankind's initial social condition. Human nature just dictates to us as it does and it does so innately, so that perceived distinctions between the elite and the vulgar can never be ferreted out by bloody revolutions. All that violence accomplishes is to replace the tokens within the types. Secondly, I would disagree with anyone who claims that teaching the populace to read and write, or of universally stamping out illiteracy, is equivalent to educating them. Literacy does not educate people, it merely primes them for the acceptance of popular prejudice on a larger scale than ever, readies them for what we usually refer to as the reigning ideology. If anything changes at all it is the nature of the state of false consciousness that enslaves the many; it forces them to articulate, or to parrot what they think they know."

Josh signaled the waiter for another round of drinks. He took a deep breath, resisted looking at his watch again, and said to me in all seriousness:

"Stephen. Hello? You are Stephen Lattimore, are you not? The kid who went to school in New Haven with me? Your parents had a business, did they not? They shuffled real estate around, not for a corporation, but for their own profit. They died, tragically. And you are living recklessly off the proceeds of the sale of that business, doing so against the advice of all your friends. Stephen, you are merely sitting on your ass. Do you want to put your head up there, too? Hasn't anyone told you this before?"

"Yes."

"Who?"

"The women I date, mostly."

"Well then?"

"I don't think that the history of how I got to be where I am has anything to do with my writing. And I am not 'sitting on my ass.' I am idle."

"What's the difference?"

"I am not simply holding back from leading a life style like yours. I am living at the top."

"Oh, come on, Stephen! This is absurd."

"I disagree."

"Are you telling me that your life *style* is better than mine? Better than the one Jane and I plan to lead?"

"If you put it that way, yes."

"Living in idleness until your parents money runs out?"

"True enlightenment begins and ends in idleness."

"I see. Idleness is, then, a full time calling."

"It is. It takes discipline, patience and perseverance. It is not a state that can be turned over to the many because the many can not tolerate it."

"I am one of the many? A member of the corporate mob?"

"You are a worldly man, Josh. We were speaking about the prejudiced masses."

"Oh, do continue about them."

"They are an aggregate of souls whose collective spirit is one of reaction taken as action and who perceive everything, including their own religious beliefs in a material sense. For them, a cleric holds spiritual sway because he is in charge of a tall building."

"Masses of people have been educated since the French Revolution, Stephen. You have to admit to that. There is universal literacy being practiced, is there not?"

"Those whom you call the literate public inevitably confuse schooling with school buildings. They confuse their education with their own homogenized socialization, never realizing that they are being controlled by an intelligence utterly foreign to their own, as surely as were the peasants of Condorcet's day. It is a farce."

"Tell me, my suddenly self-appointed aristocratic friend, are you just speaking about schooling in rural states, or do you include undergraduate education in the Ivy League as well?"

"If the shoe fits."

"What the hell does that mean?"

"I have just gone on, since my parents death, to acquiring true education is all. You might say it has been . . . thrust upon me."

"Really."

Josh laughed depreciatingly and sat back in silence until our refills arrived. Then he added:

"All you did was trade in one set of tall buildings for a single tall building. Your precious Medallion Club. Where does you 'higher education' come into play, through the service entrance?"

Josh chucked at this but he was clearly angry at what he took to be my newfound pretentiousness. I returned him my most gracious smile.

"True, the building I am living in is a grand one. The facilities are first rate. I like it."

"For example?"

This question threw me. I said, quite stupidly:

"Ah? There is free coffee served in the afternoon when one comes in to read the New York Times."

Josh started to laugh, then checked it and looked at me as if he felt sorry for me of a sudden.

"You are serious about this stuff."

"I am."

"Grab your drink. Let's go in to dinner. I want to hear more."

We sat down in the main dining room and ordered a bottle of Medoc, a country pâté, mixed green salads and while I got the fillet mignon with port wine sauce, Josh ordered the rack of lamb with caramelized onions. We said little until we had chugged down our second drink. Then the wine arrived and I started in all over again. I don't know why I felt defensive with Josh. In college we always hated people who could not come down off their high horse, so to speak, and be regular fellows. Was I playing that role now? If I was, then to hell with it! I don't know why I was bowing to Josh's uninformed opinion of me and why I was made to feel suddenly ridiculous. Yes, "ridiculous" was the right word for it. I felt, as well, as if I could at any moment break out in a laugh and start asking Josh to get me a job at The Hartford. But that was absurd. It was also the ridiculous, the comic and the banal. In any case I felt compelled to go rushing ahead with my words. Of course they now sounded pompous in my ears as well, something that would never happen to me while I was alone. I felt bad even while telling myself that people like Josh Rider have no interest in topics that are broadly intellectual, let alone subjects of true, focused contemplation, be they practical or theoretical.

"I was defending idleness to you. I don't know why but I was. Let me put it this way. Aristotle was on to something when he wrote that while the masses run out and grab up all the necessary jobs, a few people do hold back and it is they who eventually grasp onto what makes life sufficient for all mankind."

"I take it that law is a necessary and not a sufficient job. I take it that what you do at the Medallion Club in the wee hours is not necessary but does suffice."

"You take it right in both cases."

"What is the point, then?"

"The point to be gleaned from Aristotle is that he simply assumed that those who sought the life of sufficiency, holding that out as a *possibility* for all mankind, were wealthy enough to pull it off! His world was not one allowing for an intermixture of citizenship and poverty."

"That is all very nice, Stephen. But didn't we start with a Frenchman and not a Greek?"

"All right. To return to the Marquis de Condorcet, I feel that what really happened in the world following his attempt at revolution is this:

we have maintained a dichotomy between the educated elite and prejudiced masses but we have let slide Aristotle's strict rule of Greek citizenry while doing so. A small number of people have assumed elite, educated, idle roles in life without having any idea of how this is to be paid for or, more to the point, who is going to pay for it."

"Well, now we are getting somewhere. What are you doing about this little financial problem of yours? Living the way you do you are going broke are you not?"

"I will be broke soon enough."

"And?"

"Certainly it will not do to ask for financial support either from friends or from strangers."

"What, then?"

"Don't know."

"How about marrying a rich lady?"

"Don't think so."

"Why not? Others have bitten that bullet."

"It makes the wealthy ones bristle to suspect they have been drawn into some sort of crooked contractual scheme, one that they did not sign for, that they did not approve of, and that they do not like or respect."

"What are you now, a preacher for morality? This is new to me, Stephen. Yet it is beside the point in any case. Just tell me this: what the hell are you planning to do three years from now when your money is gone?"

"I don't know, really."

Josh fell silent. He frowned. He looked thoroughly irritated. This look was broken into, from time to time, by a burst of laughter, one that betrayed the sort of exasperating feeling he must be having towards me. I maintained what I hoped was a dignified look. Josh ended the silence right after we hoisted our first toast of red wine to one another.

"What else do you write down at your desk, Stephen?"

"I report on my dreams."

"Your dreams."

"Yes. I seem to dream only during my afternoon naps and never while sleeping after writing; I suppose I have effectively wiped the slate clean once I leave my desk just before dawn. Yet my napping dreams do fascinate me and I never fail to record them."

"You live a life of idleness and yet you nap, too?"

"Yes. I only sleep from six a.m. till ten a.m."

"Why?"

"From ten a.m. till three I am involved with my idleness and then with my lunch."

"You take a five hour lunch?"

"No, no. I merely exist until around noon and then I go eat. Lunch itself runs about three hours. Then I nap from three in the afternoon until six p.m. So you see, I only sleep seven hours a day."

"If you add it up."

"I am concerned with idleness again, and with my supper, from six p.m. until midnight. Fussing and taking my time and . . . as I do with lunch."

"You eat by yourself mostly?"

"Mostly."

"Stephen, I . . . don't know what to say."

"It is part of the proper life for mankind, you know . . . unless you are a waiter or an employee of some sort. It sounds silly when I talk about it with you but . . . in *practice* it makes a lot of sense. It makes sense to me, anyway. And it is exhausting! I hardly go out except to eat. This life I lead consumes me."

Josh blew softly into his glass of wine and the hum carried across the table to my ears. He seemed to be looking into that glass intently. He said, almost in a whisper:

"You were telling me about your dreams. What did you dream about during your last nap?"

"I dreamed that I was living alone in the desert and had been doing so for years. I don't know why I was living in the desert; for some reason I felt that I had been insulted and that I was there thanks only to having been insulted, though I could not remember just who it was had done me this wrong. All I did know was that this insult festered inside me and that I bore it like a physical pain."

I stopped just here but Josh said nothing. So I continued.

"My insult had, in fact, caused me to analyze the nature of insults in general. That is what I did all alone in the desert. I thought about what a single, unkind word or action, or accident can do to a person's soul. I measured the gulf that was created, as the result of an insult, between the victim and everyone else in the world. I say everyone else, for the victim of an insult is removed from the society of all persons and not just from the society of the perpetrator of the insult. That is the real extent of the damage. I was not only alone, I was not only condemned to analyze my own damaged thought patterns so that my only course of life was to stare down, down, down into my own self, I was to the point where I was able to convince myself that such analyses were not only fruitful but that they were good, too. Good for me; good in principle. We are all victims of painful insult, are we not? We are all damaged souls. What better thing can we do than to go off by ourselves and live alone in the desert, licking our wounds not so much to heal them as to keep them moist and festering."

"If you say."

"While I was living in this reclusive, festering state of insult I happened to turn on the television set in my hermit's room and there was a professional prize fight taking place. I was drawn to this fight, as I would be to any sort of innocent recreation. What I witnessed amazed me. One of the fighters . . . these were heavyweights . . . suffered four insults in the course of a three-minute round. He was struck below the belt, elbowed in the ear, head butted and thumbed in the eye. Each time he was physically abused like this he appealed to the referee who only shouted: "Come on! Fight!"

"When the bell rang the fighter returned to his corner and complained to his second but his second only slapped his face and said: 'Forget about it. You're in a fight! Get busy.'

"My dream was a long, complicated one and I guess it was interrupted by periods of deeper sleep. I am not sure, however. Perhaps I had two separate dreams. In any case, I dreamed, during this same nap, that whatever it was that allowed me to live alone in the desert without financial worry was suddenly taken away from me and I had to move out of my cozy surroundings and go into the city make a living. I had to make a living by grubbing away as a grocery clerk. It was a busy, meaningless and demeaning job and one that I thoroughly hated. It was no longer the case that I could lick my wounds and worry about insults the origin of which I was in the dark about, it was the case that I was getting shoved around in countless petty ways.

"Then one day, who should walk into the grocery store but that same boxer whom I had seen on television being four times insulted. I followed him out of the store, accosted him and I told him what I had witnessed from my place in the desert. The boxer confessed to having no clear memory of these four fouls. Once more, he dismissed them as being of little account.

"'I can't be dwelling on no insults, as you call 'em,' he explained to me. 'Life always be handin' us insults. Life itself is one great big insult. I was too busy makin' a living. I made a good living. Now I am retired and I cool out on the desert. I like it out there. I couldn't put up with the sort of life you lead here in town; that is what I call bein' really insulted.'

"That is when I woke up. Strange, no?"

Josh looked around helplessly. He seemed to be wrestling with his conscience for a while, and then snapped to attention. He had made up his mind about me.

"I find your work very fascinating, Stephen. You have some good ideas. Maybe the next time I am in New York on business,we can discuss them further."

"Oh. Can we? It is so odd to hear you patronizing me, Josh Rider."

It was all over. The masks had fallen. Josh drained his glass of wine and looked at me through narrowed eyelids.

"Do you remember you used to call me a 'poor soul,' Stephen?"

"Certainly."

"Who is the 'poor soul' now, Stephen?"

It was my turn to laugh.

"That's good, my friend. That is very good. Do you remember Colette's *The Last of Cheri?* "

"No."

"It was about this idle fellow who lorded it over his busy friend for years. The friend, a poor soul, worshipped our hero at the beginning. Our hero had a superior attitude . . . even if he was, in truth, only a gigolo. Then the tables were turned. The friend went into business, found his niche in life, and ended up insulting the man he once admired. I am not a gigolo, Josh. But I ask myself; am I insulted anyway? Shall I object to the way you treat me?"

"What's the verdict?" Josh asked sardonically. He was upset, of course, but he was, already, trying to grope his way along towards the restoration of our friendship. We were, after all, genuine friends.

"I shall give you a yes and no verdict. You only have one point to bring up to me, Josh. You keep reminding me that all I have left in this world are a few shrinking dollars gleaned from my parent's awful death. Isn't that so?"

"Almost."

"What else, then?"

"I would accuse you of an unjustified arrogance, Stephen."

"Arrogance?"

"You heard me."

"I do not think I am arrogant. I think that my life style is superior to yours. That is all."

"Your life style, as you call it, will run out very soon!"

"I don't care."

"You don't care!"

"No."

"Good God, Stephen! What damage you must have sustained when your parents died. You need help. Do you know that?"

"I do not agree with you. I am doing what I am doing of my own volition and I regret nothing."

"You are going to be thrust out into the streets before you know it. You have no profession. You have no skills. You haven't got a clue about what is going on in the real world. And yet here you are, denying your own paltry sense of arrogance. I fear for your future, Stephen. I pity you as well."

"Don't waste your pity on me, man. I am capable of contemplation. I eschew mere action. I care not for circumstances."

Josh looked me in the eye. His look was earnest I will admit.

"May I tell you something, Stephen?"

"Of course."

"You are falling apart right in front of my eyes. Don't you realize that? Anyone who 'fusses' over and then eats lunch by himself over a period of five hours a day is a Goddamn mess! I am not lying to you!"

I pursed my lips and shrugged my shoulders.

"I will grant you this much and this much only, Josh. I have grown soft in this world. I readily admit it. I am only in my twenties and yet I fatigue easily these days, even with my naps. And it does occur to me that my musing over lunch and dinner somehow just wouldn't do for a busy fellow like you. Why, you said so yourself. You skip the heavy food and get right down to business for The Hartford. Have you run into Wallace Stevens there, by the way? Ha-ha. Excuse me. But you must understand, I am disciplined for a whole different way of life. I give myself to my musing. You, on the other hand, give yourself to The Hartford. Can't you see . . . in doing so you are not able to give yourself over to idleness!"

"Give myself over to idleness? Me? I just don't get you."

"Don't you, Josh? I am telling you that, just as I am fatigued to the point where I cannot live the active life, you are fatigued to the point where you cannot lead the contemplative life. I get fatigued if

I have to bring a date to a show. I get fatigued just being in the elevator, mornings, with men who are on their way to meetings dressed in suits like the one you are wearing. My whole life is a battle against tiredness if you must know. But that should not come as a surprise. The contemplative life, being best, does limit the person who lives such a life. Whenever I awaken from my musings, whenever I awaken and find myself totally thrust into space and time, I am exhausted! But you, my friend, you suffer the same fate as I do."

Josh was chewing his greens and looking everywhere but at me. When he did speak again, it was about the weather. The rest of the meal was given over to just this struggle between meaningless small talk and uncomfortable silences. Twice Josh promised to look me up again when he returned to New York, twice I promised to drive up to his spring wedding on the strength of his verbal invitation. We both feared we would probably never see one another again, for friendship can be tenacious.

Chapter Six

I was unable to drag my eyes over the pages of Jeremy Lighter's second volume of poems. No doubt this secret, ongoing series of omissions on my part was going to end up embarrassing me sooner or later; Jeremy was bound to ask me about his publications. Yet try as I may, I could not turn my attention to his work, and I knew why. When one gets down to the root of a recognizable, living human state, say one's having accrued a sense of guilt, or having become aware of the pain one suffers when one decides to go on bearing this guilt instead of seeking to rid oneself of it (and here one can think of a young Catholic conspiring to have sex against the will of God or the parish priest), one need not stop there and call that one's essential condition, or one's moral deserts; one can just keep going. One can delve down so deep into one's own inexhaustible self, temporal limitations aside, that a second level of explanation may be uncovered. This new factor, understood to be entirely foreign to what festers above, can begin to operate on our will from within a totally separate albeit fully conscious enclave that effectively renders the initial, root level, *emotional* base of our conscious self entirely moot. This was, in a word, precisely what Jeremy tried to accomplish in his writing, at least in the first volume we had discussed. He tried to render the horror of guilt moot in favor of a dispassionate appreciation of beauty. He tried to make beauty that which defined him. I suppose I was doing the same thing in my own negative way. Yet the question lingered: were we both piling straws on a camel's back?

One thing I did do was look up Jeremy Lighter's name in one of those encyclopedias of American poets at the Medallion Club library. What I read there was of little help to me. The man whose life was now linked with my own was given a page-and-a-half of fine print, the first half of which was biographical. This fact rendering told me no more than I had learned from the dust jacket of his first book, though it was told in many more words. The second half of the article discussed the technical aspects of Lighter's poetic style. I could only gloss over what was being said of these "nuts and bolts" issues, to rehash Jeremy's own phrase, but it was clear that the fellow who wrote the article was unabashedly praising Jeremy. In other words, he was a good poet. He was a serious poet. He was an upstanding example of a hard-working American writer. There was one passing reference to theft as a poetic theme of his first volume, but the thrust of the criticism was not about the substitution of beauty for guilt and, once more, this substitution did not seem to matter to the writer of the article; what did seem to matter were technical details to do with language. Images, I was told, were to be understood as linguistic achievements. There was no discussion of the direct substitution of seeing for words. So, this critic altogether ignored whatever Jeremy did see and whatever objections to this seeing I had. Which meant, to me, that Jeremy's claims of being his own aesthetic theorist were still left very much up in the air. I called him up and suggested another lunch. His answer was both cryptic and alarming.

"So you read the stuff. How are you holding up?"

"Fine."

"And the risk factor? Is the problem of the Other getting to you?"

The "Other?" Wasn't there something in the title …? I had to think fast. I had to think like a student who comes to a lecture hall unprepared. Perhaps the student did not hear what the professor had to say last time class met and, once more, failed to read the assignment for this day. This need be no cause for alarm, for there is always the possibility of drawing upon the professor's same subject matter from a universal standpoint. Sometimes a fresh and uncluttered mind will, instead of making a farce of the lecture, move the class along in unexpected and beneficial ways while those know-it-all students who have assiduously prepared will only stilt the proceedings with their small insights. Jeremy's second volume of poems was about shame first and foremost, was it not? I had forgotten about the "Other." By that I suppose he meant other people, or other minds. I could talk about that subject as well as any poet could talk about it. But what did he mean by risk and …?

"We'll talk about it, Jeremy."

We had lunch in the main dining room, and we said little while we ate. Jeremy kept looking up from his comfit of warm duck to fix me with his terrible blue stare, and I kept looking away from my veal and peppers to stare at what appeared to be a fat bulge behind the double-breasted fold of his blue blazer. The bulge in my breast pocket was smaller; in fact it was no thicker than a slice of paper, but it was altogether more comforting. Once again I patted the pocket over my heart. I kept a smile on my face.

Was I right to indulge my feeling of paranoia? Was I right to ignore this feeling? Had Jeremy and I already formed a very tense, even bizarre relationship with one another, or was my imagination overheating, and Jeremy Lighter was merely a man who had come to the club for a few days and was glad to have a luncheon companion out of his poetic set from time to time? No matter the facts, this poet and I seemed to be sliding into a relationship of sinner and confessor, though I was not sure which role had fallen to me. We finished lunch and went down to the main lounge to smoke cigars. My fear of what Jeremy would have to say to me or what he would eventually ask of me became so great that I took the initiative and tried to divert the conversation from talk of shame, the initial subject of his book, to talk of the Other, a more general if more maddening topic, while banking on the possibility that Jeremy would step in at some point and link the two concepts together in his own aesthetic way.

Yet even before I opened my mouth I noted that despite the higher level tension in the air we continued to be human animals on another level; we drew comfort from sitting together in this vast, smoky den as surely as did cat and master before a fire. Ours was an *animal* drive toward sociability that just checkmated all of our theories before they could even get off the mark. Anyway, I thought, why not start out from there?

"It occurs to me, Jeremy, that we live in a world of others as do droplets of water carried along in a common stream. We are in a river of life, if you will. We derive countless benefits from our being aligned with and adhered to the Other. We gain social and political comfort and we gain protection from the horror of being alone with ourselves. Yet while we go flowing along as a communal whole, we cannot help but notice that our social stream flows between two confining and defining banks. The first bank, which I will call the descendent bank, is where we fall to, or end up on, if we fall out of the common stream because of some moral, psychological, or physical failure. If we are beached on this bank we are as good as dead."

"And the opposite bank?"

"The opposite bank, which I will call the transcendent bank, is what many of us flowing along in the communal stream aspire to if we find this stream constraining us in some way, be it spiritually or artistically. In other words, we may come to grasp that the benefits of being in the communal stream are really hindrances. We may see that communal living is fraught not with individual sacrifice, but with the sacrifice of the individual. So we try to gain the transcendent bank. We have mystic visions; we write literary gems and the like. Yet what we eventually discover, to our chagrin, is that the attainment of the transcendent bank is every bit as deadly as is the descendent one. And here, Jeremy, comes the great discovery. It is not so much that it is paradoxical to find out that the same dangers lie on both banks; it is that the banks are one and the same!"

"What, then?" Jeremy asked, his eyes riveted upon me and his scissors lips cutting into his tightly packed Ashton cigar. He appeared to be genuinely, even intently interested in what conclusions I might draw. So, like that unprepared student who happens to strike a chord in the class, I went boldly ahead with my extemporaneous speech, hoping that the poet would consider my words an oblique critique of his poetry and take up the cudgel from there.

"What we must do, once we make the discovery that leaving the stream for any purpose is fatal, is to realize that our human identity is more influenced by misunderstood existential factors than it is by our grasp of our own human essence. Most people get bored, Jeremy. They get bored being with others. Yet they get bored being by themselves, too. All men, that is, except me, ha-ha."

"All men except you?"

"That's right."

"You are never bored?"

"No. I live alone and I like it. I have given boredom up."

"And the Other?"

"I do not have any *philosophical* problem with the Other. What I am denying is the universality of an existential condition called boredom. I can bear certain things. I say so shamelessly. Which brings us to your theory of shame, does it not?"

From the look on Jeremy's face and from the way his body suddenly seized up, I knew my words had hit the mark. I felt safe now. I was even in a position of knowing I would be able to offer a critique of whatever it was Jeremy was going to say to me before he actually said it. I sat back in my leather chair, puffed on my own Ashton, and listened to Jeremy, who carried on in his loud voice.

"In my first volume of poems I dealt with guilt and beauty. I learned to look at the very environment in which we live and I managed ... not so much to deny the environment, which would be madness ... but to change it in some radical way thanks to my own powers of vision. I saw it as less, then as more. I found beauty in the reduction.

"In my second volume of poetry, I dealt with the issues of shame in relation to other people, or what the Germans call the *Mitwelt.* But you know all this, Stephen. Right?"

"Yes, and, I would hazard to say that bearing shame is worse, for you, than bearing guilt."

"Oh, yes. Yes. More importantly, it is radically different!"

"I would agree with you there. But that is not enough for the purposes of our conversation today. It is not enough for you to prove or even for me to assent to your argument that the look of another human soul can penetrate through our skeptical fog so that we *know* there are other minds and that our *knowing* this is thanks to our being shamed by the look of the Other. As I said, I am not interested in this or any other philosophical argument to do with this issue. What interests me, what interests you I dare say, are those childhood beginnings that lead you to these truths. That, and the aesthetic twist you gave them ..."

"To my own peril."

"Exactly."

Jeremy let his breath out in tiny dribbles. I was not sure whether he was laughing softly or sighing painfully. He considered me with a sidelong glance and then said, in his booming voice, "The thing is, Stephen, you have started us off on such a high, abstract plane that I hesitate to ..."

"To what?"

"To plunge us back into the singularity of anecdote."

"Feel free to do just that."

Jeremy made this little breathing noise again. I think he was frightened and was trying to laugh in the face of his fear but making a poor job of it. His flint-blue eyes looked away into an indistinct distance.

"We were a group of boys out for a lark. We were, I don't know, not quite teenagers. In our early teens."

"Are you harking back to Augustine again?"

"No! Ah, no. We are through with him. This is about the long road down to feeling shame. There is an element of theft in the initial story, but it has not to do with theft. You should be put on guard about that."

"Go on."

"We wanted to bond, to rebel, to do whatever boys do when they are out on a lark. One kid broke a window, one kid sliced some clotheslines, and one kid peed into the back seat of an automobile. It was my turn to do something bad. So I said, 'I'll steal something.'

"We were running though a bit of woods at the time, and at the edge of those woods, along the main thoroughfare, there happened to be a fruit stand. Someone got the idea that I should steal a watermelon for the whole group to eat while lazing about in those woods. I agreed. I went down to the road and looked at the situation. There was a low fence about the front of the fruit stand, one that came roughly to my waist. The watermelons were piled up in the open behind this fence but outside of the closed fruit stand itself. The pile was brilliantly lit with spotlights. I could not very well climb into the enclosure; I would be exposed as if up on a stage. So what I did was this: I leaned on this low fence and tried to stretch myself out to where I could reach the watermelon lying closest to one corner of the stand. The fence was flexible, being made of mesh, and soon I was stretched out nearly parallel to the ground. I was lying, stretched out, for a long while since my fingers could not quite grasp the nearest melon. My fellows, safely hidden in the woods but able to see me from an angle, kept whispering loudly, encouraging me to wiggle my way farther along this softly supporting fence. The traffic was passing along the road, and people were looking over to where I lay suspended as if on air. Finally I wiggled backwards, stood up, and rejoined my fellows in the woods, empty-handed. They demanded to know what had gone wrong.

"'I am exposed to the whole town,' I explained. 'All of you did your deeds in secrecy; I was laid out for viewing. I can not conduct myself that way.'"

"You felt shame because those driving by looked at you?"

"No. That was the curious part. I did *not* feel shame, then; I only felt *exposed.* In fact, I was vaguely upset because I did not feel horrid."

"What did you feel?"

"Not much. I just knew that what had happened to me was merely the *exposure* to the look of the Other."

"How does this differ from what we are here to talk about?"

"Mere exposure to a look, without the accompaniment of shame, only operates as a mere sanction. It is like a policeman standing on a street corner. It is like a surveillance camera grinding away, nothing more. Why, people like Mill are right when they say that sanctions internalized, even to the point of religious fervor, are no better or worse than external sanctions properly imposed. They fit the bill of utilitarian morality but leave us untrammeled down in our souls."

"What, then? What are you telling me?"

"I am telling you that the inspiration for my second volume of poems did not come directly from childhood but was merely set up there and kept on hold. The inspiration did come, of course, and when it did it was infinitely more painful to me than was the pain of guilt. But one must actually feel it; one cannot simply be 'caught in the act,' so to speak. Do you follow me?"

"I think I do. I think what you are saying is true of the reader, or of the listener as well."

Jeremy shook his head impatiently.

"No. What you are getting at, Stephen, is the problem of shame being converted into *words*. Dostoevsky, for example, is a master of portraying shame and of conveying this horror to his readers. Think of Titular Councilor Golyadkin bursting into a party unannounced in *The Double*, or of Luzhin trying to discredit Sofya in *Crime and Punishment*. Why, even I was overcome with discomfort reading these melodramatic scenes. But when I return to them now, and look at them word by word, nothing happens to me. It is all technique."

"Touché. Nevertheless, Jeremy, it is time to tell me how you progressed from the mere exposure to the look of the Other to the hideous shame that drives your aesthetic life."

At this juncture, I ran through a few technical niceties gleaned from the encyclopedia article. Jeremy nodded excitedly, being completely taken in by my approach. Then he rushed on.

"When my first volume of poems was favorably received by the critics, I was honored by a party hosted by some friends of mine from my undergraduate class. They rented a large house on Long Island, and dozens of luminaries were invited to a garden party. One of my friends had just been to India and he had hanging about him, as I put it then, a short, dark, Indian fellow who was here in the States and working in a convenience store, as I remember it. The man was once a taxi driver in India, and my friend had hired him as a guide. Now he was, I don't know, doing the little man a favor or something. Anyway, the Indian was staying with my friend, and he tagged along to my triumphant party. To this party was invited Summerville Ernst, the man who was then one of the more successful trade publishers in America. A tall, haughty patrician of a fellow, he came late to the party in a chauffeur-driven Rolls Royce, and when he was disgorged from this, he came forward, hand out, and was immediately gracious and kind to me. Then he grasped me by the elbow and told me to introduce him to everyone standing on that rolling green lawn. People just naturally fell into one long line; it was as if we were receiving Summerville. It was as if he was royalty. I went down this line with him and introduced him to one person after another. The man kept his hand out and shook every hand in that line, remaining gracious and outgoing and yet haughty and aristocratic the while. Now at the end of the line, at the very end of the line, stood this little Indian fellow. He was smiling and his chest was puffed up and his hand was out and ready to be shook. He was ready to shake hands with this mighty publisher. And then my downfall came.

"I introduced Summerville Ernst to every single person on that lawn except for the little fellow standing last in line. But Summerville only tightened his grip on my elbow and said, 'And here? Introduce me here, why don't you? What is the matter with you, Jeremy?'

"I did so. I was not gracious about it myself. I just pointed at the little fellow and mumbled his name. For his part, the little Indian kept to his good spirits, and Summerville was especially gracious to him, not only shaking his hand but exchanging many pleasantries with him while holding fast to my elbow. And as for me, I was finally and suddenly plunged into shame, and I felt this horrid sickness in my brain, and my chest was constricted and my eyes tried to look away, but wherever I turned, all I could see was the brave little Indian fellow keeping his smile even when I failed to introduce him. You see, Stephen, I had ... I had acted like some sort of class-conscious snob, and for that I was crushed by the look of the Other. And this whole world of the Other, of the *Mitwelt* came crashing into my soul, and I tell you it has never left it. It never goes away. I bear it during every waking moment of my life along with my guilt. I bear all this guilt and all this shame, and I bear the reality of the environment and the reality of the Other, and I am crushed. And I am staggered. And I tell you, that until I was able to divert some of that pain through the writing of my poetry I could scarcely see myself as going on living with such a weight to bear."

Jeremy stopped speaking. I gave him a few moments to compose himself, and then I bore in upon him, perhaps mercilessly.

"Excuse me, but are you trying to make the same point as before?"

Jeremy frowned. Perhaps he was expecting a rush of sympathy on my part, or perhaps he expected me to squirm for him. But I was caught up in the poetry that I had not read and in a theory of aesthetics I had not invented.

"What's that?"

"You are the one offered the example of Dostoievsky, Jeremy. I think we agree that words, written down on a page can, in some circumstances, raise all sorts of strong emotions in the soul of a reader. Not so upon rereading perhaps, but during the initial reading. The reader is made to *feel* what the writer once felt himself; there can be no doubt about that. And there can be no doubt that what the writer is doing is *using* his feeling, of shame in this case, to produce his written art. The writer is deliberately setting aside shame in favor of something that may be considered of aesthetic beauty. Shame *as* beauty: Will that suffice? But you, Jeremy, made a very different claim regarding your first volume of poems. You claimed that you actually did see the dark at day. Yet here you are saying that you were merely reacting like a good writer and not seeing the world differently than the rest of us."

Jeremy nodded his head and answered me directly.

"You make a good point. Yet I will not disappoint you. I saw the world of the environment changed as a child dealing with guilt and I saw the world of other souls change when I was consumed with shame. I did so. I tell you I did."

His voice sounded petulant at the last. Neither of us had anything to say after this. We went on puffing our cigars quite self-consciously. If Jeremy was being serious with me, and I am sure he was, this raised the possibility that I was speaking to some sort of psychopath. For how could a man be a visionary . . . twice . . . without being absolutely mad? He had, I recalled, already mentioned that it would be madness to *deny* one of these worlds, but to change one for oneself? Finally, I tried to put the train of this entire conversation into some sort of short order though I am not sure that what did come out of my mouth accurately fit that bill.

"What you are claiming, Jeremy Lighter, poet, is that you have seen not one, but two worlds altered in your own sensual and intellectual sights. In the first instance you saw the dark at day. But in the second instance . . . what? This is what you must tell me. I cannot find it in your poems or on the pages of your book or amongst the many letters that go into making up your words. Even your story of feeling shame, though it comes across to me with perfect clarity, does nothing to convey this extraordinary claim you just made.

Furthermore, you have admitted, for the first time, that both guilt and shame do sit heavily upon your soul and despite your poetic, or I should say, aesthetic transfers. You have converted some of what you *feel*, some of what you *bear* and some of what you *suffer* into the nuts and bolts of your poems. You differ in no wise from other writers in doing so. You don't seem to appreciate, much less to revel in your sensitivity as a poet. No doubt you, like Robinson Jeffers, feel that suffering puts the animate creature on the bottom rather than at the top of the scale of living values. But let us set all of these considerations aside. Let us set watermelons and handshakes aside as well. Now do tell me: you saw the world in which we live, the world that surrounds us with its space, time and matter go dark in the midst of day and then you saw it return to a double light; what did you see when you felt shame regarding the world of the Other? You must have *seen* something and not just *felt* something that could be described in words. Isn't that the case, Jeremy?"

The man hesitated to answer this time. I knew he would. For the odds of his having seen the world of the Other transformed, by shame, into an entirely different "light," to press the metaphor of metaphors, seemed more prohibitive, to me, than did the odds of his winning a thirty seven million dollar lottery drawing. And, if Jeremy "won" this one, I might consider him mad for sure. A waiter happened by to see if we needed service from the standing bar and I ordered us both gin and tonics. This transaction allowed my friend a few minutes to consider his words. When he did speak, he seemed, and remarkably so, to have recovered his booming voice and his bonhomie attitude. He had recovered his bold, blue-eyed look and his blood letting smile as well.

"You said, Stephen, you were not concerned with the philosophical issue of other minds. Fair enough. And you make it clear that you are not going to be satisfied with either the use of words to evoke meanings and feelings, or with general uses of metaphor to do with seeing what one feels. But in denying me all of this you leave me no choice in the matter. You are asking me, straight out, if I can see a man's soul. You are asking me if I can see a man's soul when he shames me. Is that what you are asking?"

"You are on the money."

"If I tell you that I can see a man's soul as surely as I can see his nose . . . that I can see a man's soul directly and write about it . . . that I do not merely write poetry to convey an image of the soul unseen . . . what will you say to that?"

"What could or should I say?"

"Stephen . . . think of the opposite approach to darkness. Think of mystic flight. Think of shedding both the environment and the individual mind, too. Think of the source. And, on the return to the environment, know that your mind and other minds are returned into the bargain."

I looked at him and said flat out:

"I might buy the dark at day but I will never buy mysticism, even as an explanation. Contemplation, yes, but nothing further."

Jeremy's eyes flashed; he took a deep breath and said to me between clenched teeth:

"Perhaps you ought better say that you believe me about the dark at day but not about the *souls* of other people. Perhaps you do allow me the first vision based only on psychological factors you consider somewhat common but disallow me the second vision based on psychological factors you consider not only uncommon but downright abnormal."

"Yes, well, now that I think about it, Jeremy, if we can remove the spiritual light from the sensual world, then I suppose we can remove the sensual light from the spiritual world. But to *see* that which is shapeless, colorless, bodiless and. . . ."

"Bodiless?"

"OK. There you go. What is it like to see that, Jeremy?"

"You read my poems, did you not?"

"To hell with your poems. Tell me straight. What is it like to see a man's soul? Don't give me anything like 'the form of the living body' just here. Tell me . . . what is seeing a soul like?"

"Painful."

"To hell with that, too. What do you see? What do you see? Look at me, Jeremy. What do you see? What is the secret of *my* soul?"

At this point the most extraordinary thing happened. Jeremy took out his fat revolver and placed it on the leather couch before us. The waiter happened to be coming over with our gin and tonics and I scrambled to lay a piece of the New York Times over the gun. I was unable to find my tongue for some minutes after the waiter left. When I did speak I was fairly stuttering.

"What? Are you . . . c-crazy or something? What is the matter with you, Jeremy?"

I looked up and into his eyes. I became caught up in his terrible, flint-blue stare. I could not tell whether his eyes were filled with fury or amusement. Then the man said to me:

"I have one bullet in the gun, Stephen. The other five chambers are empty. Would you like to play Russian roulette with me? Winner takes all?"

My blood ran cold. Despite myself, I patted the outside of my breast pocket. The worst of it was . . . I actually considered his proposal and nearly said the word "yes." But then a hideous flood of anger filled me and I said to Jeremy in a guttural voice:

"If you don't put that thing away this instant I shall have to call someone."

Jeremy snorted and then put out his hands with a plea for patience. He spoke earnestly to me.

"I am going to ask you to wait for the whole of my aesthetic story to unfold, Stephen. Oh, I won't spin it out today. We have both gone through too much today. I am asking for you to bear with me over these next few days. There are other considerations to discuss. There are other emotions we have to deal with and there is one more entire world we have to face. I beg you . . . give me your time. You give me your time and I will finish telling you about my aesthetic theory."

All I wanted, that moment, was to flee Jeremy Lighter's presence. So I agreed to being patient with him and to meeting with him in the near future. He put the revolver away without its being seen by anyone else in the room and we parted at once.

Chapter Seven

Jeremy took the stairs down to the lobby and I took an elevator up to the eighth floor. We did not say good-bye and we did not look at one another while parting. I could not say anything to Jeremy even if I wanted to; I just wanted to get away from him at once. My hands were shaking uncontrollably. I made up my mind then and there to pack my bags and exit the Medallion Club for a few days . . . if not forever. I had intended to stick close to Jeremy Lighter until he gave his literary luncheon talk; I had intended to penetrate down into the core of his very being (or should I say his very strange, aesthetic being); and I had intended to be faithful, in the end, to my own scruples. I was still an honest man. That is the truth. Yet . . . the sudden display of that fat revolver and the very suggestion that Jeremy and I play Russian roulette . . . "Winner takes all" . . . appalled me. How could the man display such temerity in the main lounge of the club? It was outrageous. It was unfathomable. It was simply not done. I was actually mumbling to myself as I rushed down the corridor to my room. "I'll move into the Grand Hyatt right now. I won't tell the desk where I'm going . . . I'll just leave until Jeremy Lighter is gone back to Virginia. I will."

I fumbled with my room key but my hands shook so badly I could not get my door open. I was in a cold sweat as well.

"I'll go straight to California. I don't give a damn. I'll be out of here and I can mail him the ticket and I can . . . go to California. I can sit by the sea and. . . ."

Then I lost it completely. For the door swung open without my doing and I screamed:

"Don't shoot!"

It was Judy and she was standing there stark naked.

"Hi, Stephen. What are you on about? And what are you staring at me like that for? Do you think I'm a ghost?"

"I . . . Miss Knoffer!"

We spent the balance of the afternoon in one of my two beds.

We returned to that same bed several times for the remainder of that week, too! I was used to conducting brief affairs here at the

Medallion Club but Judy's sudden, unexpected and apparently constant attentions threw my life style into disarray. I needed to sort out my thoughts. Oh, do not misread me: I loved this particular affair! I was awash in a sea of sensual delight; my body had not felt this good in years; we were pleasing and pampering and pawing at one another in breathless wonder. Judy (who was taking vacation days) was every bit as sexy while in action as she was while sitting behind her desk clerk's counter looking good. I was not complaining one bit. It was just that it became impossible for me to put in my usual six-hour stint at my desk from midnight till six a.m. because Judy was asleep in my arms during this time slot. Our take-in breakfasts in bed lasted from nine a.m. till noon and we were back lovemaking, lounging and laughing until it was dark on the streets of Manhattan. She even made me stay awake through my naptime! Then we were out on the town. Judy liked Broadway shows. It made sense. If you grow up in the mid-west where the only performances you see are in a church, then you move to Hempstead and go to Hofstra to major in management, what else do you do with your free time than bus it into Manhattan and pay ninety bucks a head to watch a show where they sing and dance *sans* any attempt at story, drama or serious acting? And why shouldn't you think that is the cultural thing to do? But I digress.

I had, first of all, to sort out Judy's abrupt turning in my direction. We did not discuss this with one another right off; we were too busy locking lips and limbs. Judy was magnificent! Her breasts were outsized for her body. Her waist was small and her hips wide; she had long, strong legs and skin as smooth and as unblemished as fresh cream. She smelled like an endless cup of warm jasmine tea. For my part, I did not make the mistake of looking a gift horse in the mouth . . . I asked no questions for the first forty-eight hours. Then, little by little, I began learning about my bedmate, beginning with her invective towards Adele.

"That bitch? That maid who does your room? You realize the nerve of that woman, Stephen? She watches me."

"Come on, babe. She just has a way about her is all."

"No! I mean it. When I am coming down the hallway, alone, or with you, that sleazy bitch gives me the evil eye! I swear it! Who does she think she is? It's as if . . . it's crazy. Does she think she can intrude on people's lives just because she goes in their rented rooms to clean them? I mean. . . ."

I couldn't tell Judy that Adele had some reason to be jealous. How could I even broach such a subject? How could I explain to the one young lady I had my sights on since I lived here at the club that I am, and naturally so if it comes to that, not above putting out vibes (do they still use that word?) to any and all females who happen by or wander into my sprayed territory.

The Adele problem was only a minor consideration. What was the *Judy* consideration? That was what interested me enough to keep me staying at the Medallion Club even while knowing that the poet down the hall carried a revolver as surely as I carried his winning lottery ticket. I had abandoned any and all thoughts of fleeing; California has earthquakes anyway.

Judy, when she did begin speaking of her motivations, showed that she was every bit as confused about what she was doing in my bed as I was. So what began as a search for this answer led us into a discussion of any number of topics, including the reason I was staying in this room!

Judy was not sure whether she had overthrown her deeply ingrained middle-class values for a wild ride on my side of the fence, or whether she had come over to what (she thought) I did only so that I would come to consciousness about the error of my ways. Did she see me as practicing sloth, demonstrating a lack of ambition and giving my self over to corruptness? I hoped she was not going to suggest that I, too, get into a management-training program and end up serving the very people I now represented in my idleness. Judy said nothing like this. Her attacks were more benign.

"This is great living in a room like this, Stephen. But you are still so young! There is so much of life out there? You can still get at it."

"For what?"

Judy was slow to anger during those days. It was all to do with her confused strategy. She was in conflict regarding her attraction to me; that much was clear. If it was the case that Judy Knoffer had decided that she wanted Stephen Lattimore in her future, if she wanted me to be the father of her children and the cosigner on her mortgage and insurance policies including dental care and major medical, then she felt she had to change me. But before she could change a man the way a woman does change a man she had to find out what made me tick.

"You cannot go on lazing away in a single room for the rest of your days, Stephen."

"Well. Yes. The problem with that is, first of all, that you are right. No one can go on lazing about in one room for the rest of their days. It is unthinkable. But . . . or in the second place . . . that is not what I am doing."

"Not lazing about? That is what you have been telling me from the day you met me! You tell me that you are idle. You tell me that you are lazy. You tell me that you are, ah. . . ."

"Living off the money I got when my parents were killed in a car crash."

"Well, yes. I'm sorry."

"Don't apologize. What you say is true. What I told you was true. But when I say idle, when I say lazy, I have lofty meanings in mind."

"Oh, please!"

That is as far as we got with my most intimate theme of living that day. Judy was slow to anger it is true; but I was pressing upon her most sensitive button. We went back to lovemaking. Later on, when she had returned to a better mood, I suggested, half playfully, half seriously, that she join me in my version of laziness on a permanent basis, or for as long as my money lasted. All I suggested to Judy, really, was the first half of her own confused disjunction.

"If you think that what we are doing here is me; why not throw everything over and join me?"

"But for how *long,* Stephen?"

"You never know. We might be out on the sidewalk before we can blink or we might just grow old together having Chinese take-out in."

"What does that mean?"

"It means that lazing about for the rest of our lives, according to what you think lazing about means, is a moral issue at bottom."

Of course, Judy had no idea what I was talking about. How could she? What I was talking about was something known by only one or maybe two people. That was as close as I could call it. Still, it was interesting to peek in Judy's own morality closet.

"Sometimes people say things like: 'What if.' What if you had the chance to do nothing for the rest of your life? What if you had the chance to live in a room in a luxury building and do nothing? Would you do just that? Would you do nothing? Would you? I mean do nothing!"

Judy either did not grasp the implication of this question or she did not like the way I put it; she felt vaguely insulted having the tables turned on her. I did not blame her, really. Imagine someone who naturally rails against the idle rich and then is given the opportunity to being a member of that set given one stipulation; that they really must be idle, while, in turn, the idle rich they rail against are not really idle in the popular sense at all. The idle rich have real lives to lead. It is only the . . . call it the *'nouveau idle'* who are doing nothing. Ha-ha. Was Judy capable of grasping this key point?

"Stephen, you give me a headache asking me questions like that. I mean, I don't know, I mean . . . when your friend Josh, Mr. Rider used to visit you all the time?"

I had introduced her to Josh and they had kept up a kind of secondhand friendship. Still, I was surprised by this reference.

"Yes?"

"Well . . . he has settled down, hasn't he? He has a nice girl, Jane, too."

"His hash is settled, I suppose."

"Yes, but, you know. . . ."

"No. I do not know. What are you telling me about Josh?"

"He's going to have a nice house and all."

"Yes."

"Well he, he and his wife to be, will be happy."

"Good for them."

"No, I mean, they're going to live in Connecticut and . . . have a nice house."

"Judy? Tell me something. What would you define as luxury? How would you describe the luxurious life? Do you really think that Josh Rider will have a life of luxury?"

"Well, no, but. . . ."

"But what?"

"Well you know!"

Judy certainly sounded a wee bit more sophisticated when sitting behind that service desk down in the lobby. Not that I was faulting her . . . on the contrary . . . she had great potential. It was just that I would have to change her instead of her having to change me. I pressed my question.

"I ask you once more. What do *you* mean by a life of luxury?"

Judy took a deep breath and filled her cheeks with air and when she let them out with a great puff of noise she threw her hands out at well.

"Here! Us! What we are doing."

"What are we doing?"

"Going to bed. Being in bed. Lying in bed. Staying in bed. Not working. Not getting out of bed. Not getting out of bed unless you want to. Not getting out of bed except to have more fun elsewhere. Going to a show, I don't know. This is luxury. This is the life of luxury I suppose. What do you want me to say, Stephen?"

"What you are describing, for us, is not a life of luxury, Judy. It is the unfolding of a love affair. It is an interlude. It is constricted and limited and it is OK in itself but it is not designed to be a life in itself."

"That's what I am saying, Stephen . . . I . . . like Josh and Jane? She . . . they . . . have more than just going to bed together."

"So you think we are in agreement, you and I. About life and luxury."

"Well. I mean . . . you know."

"I guess I do."

"You do?"

"Yes. Except that we ought to throw out this house business. I will not live in a house."

"Why?

"I like living here at the club."

"But all this is . . . just a kind of dream, Stephen. Normal people don't *live* here, they only come here for a few days on business, or . . . or . . . for an affair or something. Like right after they get divorced? Stuff like that."

"I can assure you that my life is no dream. Not even a daydream."

"What is it, then?"

"It is the proper way to live. It is a life you must rigorously prepare for, a life that takes a great deal of discipline to maintain."

She looked at me and of course she laughed. Yet I still held out for her potential.

"Stephen, you . . . I . . . you are kidding, right? You are hiding out on life, not disciplining yourself for it. You got this money and . . . and you are ruined because of it."

"Is that what Josh told you."

"No! He . . . well. Yes."

"What if I told you that Josh is wrong? What if I told you that I maintain a most vigorous life style here at the Medallion Club?"

"Oh, sure."

"You want to hear about it or not?"

"I do! I do!"

"I am a writer. I write all night. I sleep less than most people and I keep a close watch on my activities."

"What are you writing? I mean . . . mysteries?"

"No. I am writing about the life."

"The life?"

"The life of one who lives this life."

"Stephen! You can't go on living like this . . . in a . . . ah . . . room!"

"Why not?"

"Because it's . . . boring! Not to mention prohibitively expensive."

I smiled my most superior smile and said to her in my most earnest voice,

"If I have learned anything in my idleness it is that I never, ever let myself get bored. It is not just that I, personally, have no serious capacity for boredom. It is, rather, that I truly believe that boredom has been oversold to the human race as being part of its existential condition. I feel very strongly about this admittedly radical view, for I can fill in my hours quite nicely and I think the rest of humanity can do as well. Just get at it. Just live like I do."

Judy got up off the bed, crossed the room stark naked and went to the window, placing a fingernail between two of her front teeth, her arm bent and her eyes half closed. She did not bite off that nail, she was not a biter, but she did assume the biting position. She had thrown in her lot with me . . . for better or worse or whatever . . . but there were limits to everything. Finally she removed the fingernail from her mouth, studied it to make sure she had not damaged it, pressed it to her lips to dry it, held that finger to her cheek and thought hard. Finally she said, tears filling her eyes:

"Stephen. Stephen? What am I to make of you? I mean . . . really. Are you conducting some sort of private comedy at the expense of the rest of the world but with the money coming out of your own pocket? I mean . . . I mean . . . there was this girl I went to college with? Her name was Samantha? Now she was . . . she had these parents who were rich? And they used to travel around the world all the time and she was in boarding school in high school? And she would go out on these dates and say to the boy things like: 'Don't you agree it a shame that many of the fine old words of our language, words like prig, are no longer in popular usage?' I mean, the boys wouldn't just laugh at her, they would not take her seriously or ask her out again. Do you know what I mean, Stephen?"

"I'm not sure. Did she mean prig, the small nail; prig, to haggle; prig, to steal; prig, being too insistent on detail; prig, a puritan masquerading as a moralist; prig, one who bothers us to death with his life style; or prig, one who shoves his own way of life down our throats when he ought to be living our life style, one that we assume is above our having to defend it?"

Judy's eyes went wide and I hastened to add:

"I'm sorry. I apologize. I don't know what got into me. But I will tell you this: You call up this Samantha person right now and I'll give her all the prig she wants."

Judy *was* slow to anger but she could be pushed over the line and I had certainly done that to her (but only because she was doing the same to me). Judy put on her robe, went into the bathroom and stayed there for a long while. I took a short nap. When I woke up again I heard the pipes singing loudly. Judy opened the bathroom door. Steam was swirling about her head.

"You want to take a bath with me, big guy?"

"Yes."

What a remarkable lady!

It was nice to be in the bath with the assistant manager of the Medallion Club. It was like getting away with something naughty. Still and all, Judy and I had landed back on square one. We were lovers but we were not *changing* one another. While I worked the pipes, making sure the water stayed steamy hot and while Judy worked the bath oils, making sure we stayed slippery, she took another tact.

"I am not saying that what you are doing with your life . . . for so long as you are doing it . . . is *wrong,* Stephen. I just want to point out that it is a life style that can only be lived by one person."

"How's that," I asked, surprised at the sharp tone of suspicion that entered my voice.

"Well . . . most people work."

"Writing isn't working?"

"No, I mean . . . yes. You know what I mean. I mean we can't *all* be living like you, now can we."

"I am not inviting the whole human race to join me here at the club. Just you, Judy."

"You are inviting me?"

"I am making you a serious proposal."

"A proposal?"

"Yes."

"Really?"

"Good Lord! Do you have to say words like 'really' and 'like' and 'you know' and 'you know what I mean!' Look, I'm sorry. Forgive me. Hit me over the head with the shampoo bottle. But listen! Are you that conventional? Or are you merely linking love and marriage? OK. That is OK. You want us to marry? That is fine with me. We'll get married. We won't worry about how much time we have together. A little or a lot, it doesn't matter. Here is what I will do. I'll rent the room adjacent to this one. We will each have our own room. I'll pay for it."

"For how long, Stephen?"

"Good question. It will be for a year, or for a year and a half, or else for the rest of our lives. It depends."

"Depends on what?"

"On my scruples."

"What!"

The most delicious comedies in life are born out of the most serious dilemmas. Did I read that somewhere or did I just make it up? All I knew for sure was that the sight of Judy sitting across from me in the bath with a foot high cone of soap bubbles rising off her head like a princess' tiara, combined with my vision of those six winning lottery numbers, just was a gas. I could turn that crown of bubbles into diamonds as sure as I could give the ticket over to Jeremy Lighter, if he didn't blow my head off first. Blowing bubbles, blowing off heads, I wondered if I could get a hold of the telephone number for that gal, Samantha. Poor Samantha. Her parents had gone away. They had gone around the world and left her all alone. And the boys laughed at her. I wouldn't laugh at you, Samantha. On the contrary, I would reintroduce all the old words. I would pile them into all my sentences for you. I would. . . .

"I'm serious, Judy. Come and live with me for a year or so and then we'll decide about the rest of our lives."

"But . . . what would I *do* all night while you are writing."

"I don't know. I guess . . . you will have to be writing in the next room."

"I don't want to write. I can't write! I *hate* writing."

"Then collect stamps or something. Manage a business over the Internet. Do something 'at home' as they say. As for the rest, why, we can go out and enjoy the Big Apple. I'll even learn to love opera recitals."

"But why can't we do all this from out of a house on the Island? This is . . . Stephen! These rooms . . . this room you live in is ridiculously small! I mean it is all right for a night or a weekend but . . . people need space!"

"I am holding out for a suite."

"But we all need . . . we have to have a yard."

"We have Central Park."

"But we need like, a sewing room and. . . ."

"We'll send out for that stuff. This is the world of *service,* Judy. Space is not a consideration. Service is what is 'happening.' Listen to me. I hate these new words. Give me 'prig' anytime. And I hate the very idea of living on Long Island."

"But people don't live in Manhattan anymore. They come into it. They come in to go to shows and . . . to work and . . . then they go *home.*"

"This is my home."

"This is not a home!"

"Yes it is."

"But you didn't grow up in a place like this."

"No. I grew up in Virginia. We had a small house, then a bigger house and then a series of really big houses. We had cars and yes, Mom had sewing rooms. She always ended up using them for storage. They smelled and they attracted mice."

"Do you love me, Stephen?"

"Love? Ah . . . yes!"

"Why do you deflect the question?"

"Do you love me?"

"I'm not sure. I think so. But you're so, I don't know, weird?"

"There you go."

"Oh, I'm sorry. I didn't mean . . . I meant. . . ."

She leaned over in the bathtub, as best she could, and gave me a soapy kiss. Then she gripped me by the ears, shook my head by my ears and, with her face lined up with mine, said:

"Stephen? Talk to me. Talk to me straight. What is going on with you? Why are you the way you are? People like you are so weird. I'm trying to love you. You have got to be honest with me."

"I am trying to be honest, always. I can give you a year here, or a lifetime. That is, if I can bear it. Oh! I don't mean if I can bear being with you. Of course I can do that. That is not an issue. But we need to consider the morality of . . . unless we can substitute the aesthetics of .

. . well . . . let me ask you a question, darling. Do you think you could learn to give up boredom the way the Buddhists give up desire?"

Her face was up against mine and her lovely cheekbones were shiny with oil and she was so sexy and she was laughing and she said:

"What the hell are you talking about?"

And I said:

"I am talking about the rest of our lives."

"Are you so sure it is not going to be boring for us sitting here in one or two rooms for the rest of our lives?"

"That is the rub, my darling. It is not going to be boring. It is the only way to live."

"But Stephen, I want children. And I want a place for them to play and I want to look into decent neighborhood schools. And I want a husband who goes outside and rakes leaves . . . and . . . loves his children"

At that I almost lost it. But I did not; I really did like making love to Judy. I was thinking about Samantha, too. Perhaps we could, the three of us, change the popular slang in America. Or at least combine the two. Imagine:

"Be cool, prig."

Then again. . . .

I must say that we came out of that bathtub with what we both felt was a reasonable compromise regarding our affair. We agreed to take a "wait and see" approach. Judy decided to continue her day job on the front desk starting the following Monday and she decided to continue as my girlfriend. She said that she was not *rejecting* my proposal of marriage; she was only mulling it over. I think she had really made up her mind to go on trying to change me and to help me get over what she thought was some sort of young man nonsense and what Josh Rider thought was my emotional damage.

Chapter Eight

A couple of days passed. During the interval, Jeremy and I met in the billiards room and nodded hello as if nothing had happened, nothing was up and nothing was wrong. The odd thing about it was that our joint but unspoken decision to just go along with the idea that there was nothing wrong did *not* seem odd. In fact, I do believe that the majority of the world's human beings conduct their affairs in just such a fashion. Couples engage in a drag em' out fight on a Saturday night and then wake up Sunday morning by being civil to one another and by never mentioning all the insults, lamps and ashtrays they hurled at one another just hours earlier. People get drunk at dinner parties with their friends, make fools of themselves and ruffle people's feathers; at the next dinner party everyone starts off on an equal footing and who knows which one of them will run with the bad manners this time out. Co-workers clash and clash again; it is only those who bear a grudge or set up a bunker mentality that turn out to be the losers over time. Even if we are determined not to forgive or forget we do both and have both forgiveness and forgetfulness thrust upon us by others. True, Jeremy had a gun and I had his lottery ticket, but when it comes to human nature and its weaknesses, what else could we do? We did not sit with one another in the billiards room but when Jeremy was passing out he stopped by my table to ask:

"How's it going, Stephen?"

"Not bad. I'm, ah, dating that administrative assistant down at the desk. Judy Knoffer?"

"Oh, yes. She's very attractive."

"And you?"

"My talk's tomorrow. The literary luncheon, do you remember? You coming?"

"Of course. I wouldn't miss it."

"You'll recognize some things. Though it's mostly a plenary talk, one geared to a larger audience."

"I understand. I'll see you there."

Jeremy waited by my table for a couple of moments. We looked at one another and then spontaneously shook hands. Jeff's flint-blue eyes blinked most appreciatively. I smiled but then looked down at my feet; I could not keep eye contact with the poet. Odd, isn't it, that these situations are not *taken* as odd.

Judy and I attended the luncheon talk together. There was a large audience including some of Jeremy's running buddies, that group of poets he met in the city twice a year. They were a grinning, head-bobbing bunch I must say; they reminded me of a pack of monks, or nuns, who come out from behind cloister walls once in a lifetime to promote a record they happened to have made and who weave and bob before their audience with the sort of enthusiasm that is, at once, recognized as both wholesome and sexless. I say that knowing all about the ferocity of the inner lives of poets, yet there it was before my eyes and I could not change what I did see. We heard Jeremy introduced by his publisher and when the poet was standing there ready to speak I felt a number of familiar sensations coursing through my body. I was anxious and cautious and as ready to flee as I was willing to stick around. I gripped Judy's hand so hard she winced and looked over at me as if to say: "What the hell is wrong with you? Are you all right?"

Jeremy's shock of blond hair and hard, glinting eyes caused many in the audience to squirm. Yet his voice, once he got going, was hypnotic and not just loud. I do not remember all he said, but I will try to report one part of his talk as faithfully as can be, though in doing so I will have to forgo most of Jeremy's conversational nuances. I will, as well, skip his opening remarks and the two bad jokes he told; I will get to one portion of what Jeremy told me was going to be the plenary approach.

"My father was not a poet but had a poet's sensitivity the way some people are not alcoholics but are nevertheless known as non-bottle alcoholics. My father never worked with words but he had some astounding visions. He never juggled meter and rhyme, metaphor and syllable count, but he did possess a rare and a precious soul. He did not write but he had a writer's imagination. He told stories, but only to me. My third volume of poems, entitled *In the way!* Is taken, literally, from a phrase out of Sartre's novel, *Nausea,* was actually inspired more by a story my father told me than it was by the Frenchman. Let me relate it to you.

"My father went to school down south at one of those grand old universities that was able to carry on the best traditions of southern gentility while managing to ignore most of the turmoil that was to be visited upon the south and the entire nation, too, less than a decade ahead. In other words, Dad went to college in the mid and late fifties. He agreed with assessments of that era made by contemporary social critics; his was an apathetic class of students with little or no political interest, no ax to grind on social questions and with no real sense of the damage ideology can cause. Back then, most people looked upon the ranting of Senator Joseph McCarthy with detached curiosity at best. They had no clue regarding changes about to happen in American society and they clung rather comfortably to their personal, if severe and puritanical moral codes of conduct.

"Dad was brought up to be quite scrupulous regarding his own moral conduct; everyone he knew on campus was more or less like himself. They went to chapel regularly and while they were not troubled by the practice of social exclusion, they did lose sleep if they said an unkind word to the kitchen help. They were not necessarily happy living with their naïveté; it was that they were often deeply troubled down in their souls while being simultaneously blasé about social conditions.

"Dad shared a room with two other fellows in his junior year. One of these young men was his best friend. They were both members of the debating team and both of them planned careers in public service. Dad did go into public service by the way; I do not know what happened to his friend. Anyway, Dad was walking down the main avenue of the campus one evening around six thirty. He was especially struck by the quality of twilight during that walk; the air had gone quite still and the sky was drained . . . not of light . . . but of a certain kind of light. There was traffic passing by on the campus but Dad didn't hear it. He felt uncomfortably sad for some reason. He felt alone. There was no rationale for this: it was one of those trying moments that come upon us all.

"As he went along he noticed his two roommates walking along together. They were heading in the same direction as Dad was but they were doing so on the opposite side of the street and they were hurrying. They were giggling and looked excited. Dad called out to them but they were hurrying so intently that they did not hear him. He picked up his pace and started to dash across the street to join them but he stopped short when he saw them turn, abruptly, into one of the university's administrative buildings.

"Dad thought this odd. It was early evening and the administrative offices closed at four thirty in the afternoon. What could they want in an empty building? He went on into that building some seconds after they did, just to satisfy his curiosity. Entering the place he heard footsteps pounding up the stairway. Dad realized that the two young men were headed all the way up to the fourth floor where were kept some offices for the student union. They were no doubt heading just there. But these offices would be closed as well. Dad followed the sound of their steps but he came along slowly and without making any noise.

"Gaining the top landing he noted that one of the student offices had a door set ajar. He walked up to it and entered. There he found his two roommates rifling a cabinet behind the old, scarred wooden desk allotted to the student representatives. What they were after were cartons of cigarettes. Let me explain.

"In those innocent days of the fifties it was not uncommon, indeed it was business as usual for cigarette companies to form alliances with major colleges and universities to promote cigarette sales on campuses through programs of free distribution of these cigarettes. Students, usually pretty girls, would be hired to stand on campus street corners or in front of large classrooms and give away, absolutely free, sample packs of cigarettes, packs with no more than four cigarettes in them. But during certain promotions entire packages of cigarettes were distributed, gratis.

"Everyone was happy with this giveaway arrangement. The universities were given money to allow the distributions on their campuses, the cigarette companies were gaining new customers and students got to smoke cigarettes for free. There were no losers, at least not within the context of Dad's era.

"On this campus the student representative for a major cigarette company happened to be a fraternity brother of Dad and his two roommates were in this same fraternity. Dad saw what was going on in that room at once. Their fraternity brother, charged with fair and equal distribution of these cigarettes, by the full pack, to the entire student body, had conspired to leave the cabinet open that evening so a couple of his frat brothers could help themselves.

"They were not out to steal all the cartons, just two cartons apiece. They had these in their hands when Dad entered the room. When they saw Dad their faces flushed. No one said a word. It was certainly embarrassing. What happened next was this: to cover their embarrassment Dad's friend and roommate took a fifth carton of cigarettes out of the cabinet and shoved it in Dad's hands. Then they all hurried away.

"Dad had never formed the intention of stealing . . . and stealing was always the worst crime in his eyes . . . and yet here he found himself in possession of stolen goods. He felt terrible about it. That odd sky that arched over him while he walked along that campus seemed to stay with him in the days ahead. It was never dark on the campus yet it was never really light. And he had those cigarettes, ten packs of cigarettes, twenty cigarettes to a pack, sitting on his bedside table. Two hundred reminders of his terrible crime and all of them wrapped up in bright red packages; it was a nightmare for him. He was consumed with guilt.

"He missed the irony of the situation completely. But that was the age! It was the university and the cigarette companies who should have been plunged into the horror of guilt for having successfully addicted a new generation of smokers. Instead, Dad was plunged into a state of guilt for having had that one carton of cigarettes thrust into his hands. He did not resist the gift but that was only the start of his misery.

"He went on to smoke all two hundred of those cigarettes. He concocted visions the while. He imagined that there was a living demon, a morally evil demon crawling down into his lungs each and every time he inhaled. Once again he missed the irony contained in his own visions; he should have worried about lung cancer.

"Dad actually lived out the rest of his life colored by that one incident from his college days. He took it to his death. He died thinking himself a thief!

"When he told me his story I was as effected by it as he was living it. I came to realize that we are all moral agents living here in crowded conditions on the earth. We implode upon one another's living space; we crowd in together with our own separate moral consciousnesses bumping into one another. Here is where Sartre's idea . . . for trees . . . comes into question for human beings. We are, as moral agents . . . in one another's way! We are all trying to be good and to get along, yet we are ever *in the way* for someone else! They are in our own way and we are in their way! Dad came to that realization the hard way; I have carried his burden on in my poetry.

"Dad had no sophisticated idea of what we could call the Other. He could not look beyond his own feelings of guilt and he still did not look beyond those feelings when he learned to live with himself again. The best Dad could do was this: he could realize that we are all suffering together on this earth and that we must, from time to time, shove one another aside so that we can go on suffering . . . on a deeper level. It was Dad's fate to feel horrible and in order for him to meet his fate he had to shove some other moral being aside. Dad was so fated, and he was filled with an overarching gray uncertainty, too. Now let me say a few words about that 'seeing.'

"My Dad claimed that he actually did *see* the sky remaining in that uncertain state. Oh, on the day he was going along the campus there were certain weather conditions in place all right; there was an unstable combination of sunlight and storm clouds and no doubt this produced a foggy, yellow and ash-gray light to appear in the sky down south. That we can all understand. That we can all experience and probably have done so. But afterwards, Dad claimed that he saw that dark and light, together, for the rest of his life. He began to see and feel like a poet who does not use words. And he passed that strange gift, or affliction on to me.

"I am a poet who employs words. I am a poet who employs visions, too. I do not just manipulate words to produce visions in *your mind;* I am not just a visionary suffering like my Dad. I see, I suffer and I write.

"I thought of my Dad after the publication of my second volume of poems. I thought of this story he told me, the story I have just conveyed to you. And I decided to write about Dad's experience using poetic language. More importantly, I decided to convert his sense of guilt . . . aesthetically. I decided to write about the *beauty* of my dad's tortured life.

"Do you find that hard to swallow? Let me give you an insider's view. Do come along. I invite you. Come on. Let's do some exploring.

"Look! There is your soul and there are the souls of other people. Now look closer, look at us getting in one another's way! We cannot get out of one another's way and we hunger for separation! But we cannot separate, for we are stuck together like droplets of water fused together in a common, morally repugnant mass."

Jeremy went on in this manner and the audience began to cough and move their feet and more than a dozen people got up and walked out of the room, some of them not even bothering to tip toe. Judy, who was with me, whispered in my ear:

"I have to go. I have to get back to the desk."

"But you have plenty of time, Judy, it's. . . ."

"Stephen! Please. This guy's not reading us any pretty poems; he's giving us a load of his personal baggage. People don't want to sit through that? Now, excuse me. I'm going. See you later. Bye."

Jeremy's audience continued to dwindle. By the time he got around to reading a couple of selections from his third volume of poems half the room had emptied. It was embarrassing. I went up to him afterwards and whispered:

"I don't know if you'll have time this evening, but, I'll be at Elaine's, up on Second Avenue, pretty much all evening. I won't bring Judy. Come along if you can."

He just stared at me. His face was a pain mask. His publisher, looking stunned but trying to make the best of it, was busy lobbying some of the club members of Jeremy's behalf. I slipped away.

I had lunch, took a good nap and I got to Elaine's around seven thirty. It was not too crowded and I managed to get a table in the corner farthest away from the entrance. I ordered a glass of Chianti and a bit of proscuitto, which I nibbled at along with some bread while letting the time go by as only I can make it go by. Jeremy showed up, alone, about eight twenty. He seemed quite calm and he smiled, exercising his scissors lips, as he sat down to join me.

"Was it that bad, my talk, do you think, Stephen?"

"No! Not at all! It was just that you took off in an unexpected direction is all. People were not prepared for it."

Jeremy did not seem overly disturbed about how his talk was received. Obviously, he valued the company of his fellow poets . . . the ones who would rather bite their tongues off than deliver a line of criticism . . . over the general (and I assume barbaric) public.

"I borrowed your droplets of water in a stream idea. I hope you don't mind."

"I'm flattered."

"I'd like to put that idea into a poem some day. I suspect it would be a very long poem. I could even, ah, snake it out across the pages in the shape of a meandering river. I could even drop some poems on the white page banks on either side of the stream. Poems of wild hope and terrible despair; poems utterly different from the one interconnected poem running through the stream and forming the stream."

"Do you think you will do this in volume five?"

Jeremy laughed and dropped a manuscript on the table, along with one of those by now familiar volumes.

"Who knows? Let us deal with these first."

"What's all this?"

"Volumes three and four."

"Oh."

"You heard about what lies behind volume three at noon today. It will give you a good start. But this manuscript, these poems that are about to go into publication . . . if my publisher ever forgives me for my talk today . . . should prove most interesting given what ideas we have exchanged so far."

"I see. I will be sure to read them."

"Have you ordered, Stephen?"

"No. Just a little snack."

"Then let's."

We studied our menus for a while and then Jeremy asked without looking up:

"I hope you haven't abandoned your girl friend tonight just because you were worried about me."

"It's all right. She had to get back to Hempstead tonight to deal with some household crisis or other. Baseboard rust in the bathroom that just has to be painted over, I think she said."

"Ah. I feel better hearing that."

He went silent again, as if concentrating all of his rational powers on the menu and then burst out, with what I took to be a false ring in his voice:

"So! You are still at the Medallion Club."

"Why wouldn't I be, Jeremy? I live there."

"I know that. But. . . ."

"What?"

"I thought you might be taking off for parts unknown."

I looked at him. He was neither smiling nor frowning; he was just fixing me with that awful look of his. Lord. I hoped that Jeremy was not going to take that revolver out here at Elaine's. I would have to cover it with my napkin. I stared at his jacket; there was no visible bulge tonight.

"Why would I do that?"

"What can I say? A young man like you, and with money in his pocket might want to get out and see the world. Get out and just keep going."

"Money? Well, I have some money. Not a great deal. I'm not the traveling type."

"It's good for your health, traveling."

"Is it?"

"Perhaps in your case, yes."

We went on like that through half the meal. Jeremy kept alluding to my health, to my reputed wealth, and to what a young man would most likely do 'in my shoes.' It was only when we had the veal and the mushrooms and the goat cheese and the roasted red peppers well down inside us that I brought the conversation back to his poetry.

"You have progressed from guilt to shame to the idea that an evil demon slips into your body. What is next?"

He looked at me and smiled.

"Think of it this way. We have progressed from the problem of the environment to the problem of the Other to the problem of . . . if you will . . . picking our own poison and housing it. There is only one world left to explore."

"What is that?"

"The world of the self. The *Eigenwelt.*"

"Is that so. What is the ego of a poet, then, at bottom?"

"It is a fiction."

We said nothing else for the longest while. We finished our entrees. We ordered dessert and coffee. Once again I looked hard at Jeremy's sport coat. This time he noticed me doing so and he smiled the way one smiles at a child.

"I'm not packing tonight, Stephen."

"Thank you."

"I am making a plea, nonetheless. I am asking you to read my as yet unpublished poems carefully. These final poems are stripped of metaphor. They are my most serious attempts to write down what it is to have direct seeing. If you have carefully followed everything we have discussed so far, you will be rewarded when reading these pages."

"I'll get right on it. The holiday is nearly upon us. I suspect Judy has some plans for us. Are you going to be around?"

"I am sticking around New York for a while. And don't worry about me over the holiday; I'm dining with members of my poetry-reading group. But do look me up when you get back to town."

I thought about flying away to Chile. It was not too late.

Chapter Nine

I finally made up my mind to read Jeremy's works. It was late morning. I brought a sandwich and some coffee to my room and climbed back into bed. Yet no sooner did I finish this light lunch and reach out for the first volume, the one I assumed was filled with poems on guilt and toys and other childish delights, than Adele banged at my door, interrupting me. I wasn't going to let her in at first but I did; after five years living at the club I had learned that it was not worth it to upset people like Adele, one of the few people I was in contact with on a daily basis. I got out of bed, put on my robe, let her in and stood standing about while she cleaned the bathroom and made up the very bed I meant to climb back into the moment she left. Adele was so jealous; with every passing day she grew the more miffed over my ongoing affair with Judy and I suppose this gave her license to be upset over the fact that I was still lounging about my room undressed at this late hour.

"You're no going out to lunch today, Mr. Lattimore?"

"Nope."

"That girl coming to be with you?"

"None of your business, Adele."

Adele proceeded noisily through her tasks, hoping to irritate me. She banged her vacuum cleaner around like a weapon and nearly tipped over my writing desk when dusting it. She complained about some of the things I'd left lying about in the bathroom but before she left she threw herself in my arms and began to emit any number of loud, grating sobs.

"It's hard, you know. It's hard to keep up," she got out between expels of choked breath. I had, for the longest while, been expecting just such an outburst from the maid and I dutifully wrapped my arms around her in what I supposed constituted a sympathetic and protective gesture. My hands patted her firm, sculptured back. She smelled of musk

"Now, now. There, there. It is going to be all right. I know you're having a tough time of it, Adele. I do."

In fact, I had no idea about Adele's life outside the Medallion Club.

"It's hard," she repeated, the tone of her voice softening. I caught a glimpse of the two of us in the bureau mirror. Adele's head was buried in my neck and her arms were rubbing up and down on my back. I suppose she was trying to seduce me with her tears. I sighed. I slowly disengaged myself from Adele and held her, gently, at arm's length.

"Now, now. We cannot have any more of that. Really. I am just getting ready to read some important, ah, stuff, today."

"That girl just wants to marry you and take you away," Adele said with her lips thrust out like a little girl. I smiled at her. Admittedly I found this scene charming. I thought of Granddad. Still, it is hard for a woman to play the coquette at fifty.

"Don't worry about me. I can take care of myself. Here. Here. Wipe your eyes on this napkin. Come on. Then you must go."

Adele did wipe her eyes on the napkin I had gotten along with my sandwich and coffee. She gathered all her cleaning materials and set them up against the door. Then she came over to where I was standing, grabbed hold of me and kissed me passionately. She kissed me only once and then she was gone.

I settled in again and began reading Jeremy's poems, attacking them the way I would the various sections of the New York Times. I am not, as I indicated, one who reads poetry as a rule or even on rare occasions. Those three serious poems I once had to get through in a mandatory English class remain mysterious vehicles for me until this day. (That was where I had heard of Robinson Jeffers, by the way, for they were his poems assigned to us.) I did not understand ninety nine percent of what was written on the pages in my hands now; I did not get the message behind the metaphors, be they simple or elaborate; most of all I did not feel a thing while reading them. My soul does not gallop to the beat of rhythms, written. I was not even moved by the few lines I *did* manage to understand.

Despite my limitations, I realized that Jeremy's work was not exceptional . . . as poetry. Knowing what I knew about Jeremy, his theories and his life experiences, was of no help to me when transferring it to his pages. I did not . . . what word could I use? I could not see, or grasp, or appreciate, or intuit, or "dig," or seize upon or have flashes of insight about anything at all while reading Jeremy Lighter's written work. You might say that Adele's tongue had just delivered more of a message than did Jeremy's talk of "vapid states of light descending" or "How condign my muted horror is." Jeremy's words were not going to convince me of anything. His words reminded me of Judy's friend, Samantha! They were not going to stand as proof of his aesthetic theory, nor were they going to serve as justification for his idiosyncratic claims regarding perception. Still, they did provide me with a few specific quotations I could refer to should he press me about his individual poems, something he had not done so far. Why had he not done so? I began to suspect that Jeremy had deliberately widened the gap between what he did in the medium of language and what he retained for his intimate and private self. What he was doing with me, I further suspected, was trying to find out if he could get me to see what he did retain, privately. He wanted to find out if there *could* be a way of seeing or even sharing the world prior to any linguistic turn being taken and without his regressing back into childhood or without his going mad in the process. I read through all the work, including the last volume of loose pages by two thirty that afternoon. I asked myself: What is my take on Jeremy Lighter?

I opted for a simple solution. I decided that Jeremy was simply relying on his native imagination to promote a theory of aesthetics, one that he claimed was both grounded in perception and layered over by an intellectual input that could, somehow, mysteriously change the nature of that ground. It was like this: if Jeremy could imagine that he was Superman, then he could fly. I did not think Jeremy could fly but I think he was trying his best to do just that. Why he was not content with just writing his poems is something I was not privileged to know. Was my straightforward judgment of the poet at once too quick and too harsh? I thought not. He was idiosyncratic, yes, but I was not ready to declare him to be either a genius or a madman. He was undoubtedly a tortured man but l could not say he had gone insane. He simply carried too much weight about in his inner being. Guilt, shame, the housing of an evil demon and this . . . I was not sure what that fourth volume of poems was telling me. I did not like or understand poetry but I could judge Jeremy's poetry. I put his work down and took a nap.

I dreamed about Timothy, the young concierge who stood before a portable wooden dais facing the door down in the lobby of the club for eight hours a day with his eyes gone blank. I dreamed of standing still like that myself. Is that what I would do once my parent's money ran out? If I could do that for eight hours a day and live here, too, I would do it! Yet I knew that was not possible. I could not make enough money to live in the club on a concierge salary. I tried, in my troubled dream, to imagine my life three years from now but all there was in my mind was a strange emptiness. I grew panicky and when I felt a hand gripping me I thought it was that evil demon and I woke up screaming.

"Darling! Darling! What *is* the matter?"

Judy was standing over me with a tentative smile on her face. She had let herself into the room and she was all dressed up. In her hand was an overnight bag. I chased my own evil demon away and calmed down except for the pounding of my heart. Why was it that I had twice ended up screaming seconds before looking into Judy's wonderful face?

"Oh! Oh. Right. Hi. I was just having a nightmare I guess."

"What about? You look awful?"

"What about? I already forgot. What are you doing with that bag? I thought we were having Thanksgiving dinner together. When is it, by the way? Tomorrow?"

"We are having Thanksgiving dinner together. We are going to visit your friend Josh Rider and his wife to be, Jane. We are invited."

"What?"

There was no talking Judy out of it. She and Josh had conspired against me. Before I knew it, Judy had packed a bag for me and soon enough we were sitting on a crowded train rumbling off to Hartford. Josh met us at the station and drove us out to where he and Jane's newly purchased home sat amidst a row of others looking just like it. Theirs was a raised ranch in a new housing development in West Simsbury.

Jane was there in the doorway ready to greet us. She was a toothy girl with beady eyes and with yellow hair as brittle as straw. She stood a good three inches taller than Josh. She was also a pleasant and likable young lady, one who kept sneaking amused looks at me. I am sure she felt she knew all my tricks. She shook my hand, rather too vigorously.

"Hi, Stephen. Welcome. Josh has told me all about you."

"Hi, Jane. This is Judy, I. . . ."

They embraced warmly.

"Judy and I have already met, Stephen."

"You have?"

"Oh, yeah. We gals have gotten together more than once down in the city."

I looked at Josh, who simply shrugged. I could see some sort of net closing in over me. When it came to projections and cases of (healthy) paranoia, Jeremy Lighter had nothing on me.

It was already past nightfall when we arrived and after a tour of the house, most of which was still unfurnished, and a supper of pasta with white wine, we settled into the den and the girls encouraged Josh and I to exchange some of the more ribald tales of our undergraduate days. This, I take it, was designed to be part of my new bonding. It was all rather stagy though I enjoyed exchanging stories with Josh and I think the girls did to. Jane showed us to our bedroom about eleven in the evening and she giggled when doing so. She tried to explain her sudden embarrassment.

"It's funny, right? You guys aren't married yet and Josh and I aren't married yet. Yet Josh and I already have a house. We are one up on you guys . . . which makes me feel like the traditionalist of a sudden. Does that sound goofy?"

Judy did not think so.

We got up early and we all helped with the turkey. While it was baking we took a walk through a nearby nature center and then we were driven to a cider mill where we bought lots of goodies to go with dinner. We sat down to eat about three that afternoon. Judy pointed out to me, not twice but thrice:

"They have a separate dining room, Josh and Jane. I mean, it's not like they have a table in their kitchen, or an all purpose room for dining and watching television, or for dining and other stuff; they have a room to go to just for formal dinners. Isn't that something?"

"They sure got lots of space in this place," I agreed. I was on my best behavior.

It was a great meal. Josh and Jane were doing everything they could to make me feel comfortable. So was Judy. In fact Judy was acting like a member of *their* family and was bending over backwards making me feel like the sole but privileged guest here in the far flung suburbs. Nevertheless, it struck me that both women seemed to be inadvertently acting out a satire on middle class life styles, and for my amusement. Josh said little. He held his strongest fire until it was time for dessert. I took a piece of pumpkin pie.

"This is the way to go these days, Stephen. Suburbs. Manhattan has just gotten too expensive a place to live."

"Nice place to visit though, right?"

"Of course it is. But patterns of living change and you ought to learn to go with the flow. This house, for instance, is a dream. The insulation, the layout, the wiring, the plumbing, why . . . it even has a wine cellar."

"Say. That is something. But tell me, do you have to go into the cellar to get a bottle of wine? There's no waiter you can call to do it for you?"

"Very funny, Stephen."

We started, completely without rancor, to discuss the joys of modern suburban living. I tried, now and again, to counter what Josh was selling with my own experiences of napping, lunching and dining undertaken with the spirit of gentlemanly idling, but whenever I did so the girls chimed into the conversation and steered it straight back to what Josh was describing as the only reasonable way to live. I kept my smile not to mention my temper but it was obvious that the three people sharing Thanksgiving with me did not feel that we were actually debating the relative values of one life style or another; they felt that they were living the way people ought to live and that I was simply damaged goods ready to be revived. I could not shake them out of this mind set and began to worry that all sorts of trapped emotions might end up wending their way up out of my gut. I did not want that to happen, though I had already figured out that my companions did. I knew a bit about human behavior after all. I kept on smiling and asked:

"Do you remember, Josh, that fellow whose course we took in ancient philosophy? One of the topics we used to talk about was . . . what was it?"

"You talking about Silverman? You mean his take on the conflict between the good life for man versus the good life?"

"Right."

"What about it?"

"Well, isn't that what we are debating here? You guys advocate the full-fledged, upper middle class life for mankind, one that is financed by a dizzying spiral of financial considerations; I advocate something different. I think we should all live in single rooms and . . . think. You want to live the way you do; I want to idle, think and write. Your plan may be popular, but my plan is simply . . . best. Length of time won't make us happier."

This little outburst brought total silence to the table. Josh tried to exchange a furtive look with Judy without me seeing it but of course I did see it. There was no use going on with this pretense. They felt I was being dishonest with them. They felt I was hurting inside and not ready to admit it. They knew I was going to run out of money staying full time at the Medallion Club and they were worried about me. Judy wanted to marry me. But for that I would have to change my ways. I was not going to be allowed to go on sitting here at the table giving a vigorous defense of doing nothing. Well, the ball was in their court. I finished my pumpkin pie and accepted a piece of mince pie. Yet these people wanted to save me more than they wanted to feed me. I thought: let them try.

Obviously they had their strategy worked out in advance. Since I was not being seduced by the joys incorporated into the walls of this raised ranch, the next step was probably their insisting I tackle that awful, nameless horror that held me in its grip. Josh finally did move in this fateful direction.

"Stephen, your parents were killed more than five years ago. God! My grandfather was killed in a car crash. And Jane's sister died in an accident. It is terrible. We all agree with that! But you have to move on! You have to get a life."

"I have a life, Josh."

"No you don't. You're hiding out! And things have gotten out of hand. I'm sorry, Stephen, but the time has come to be blunt with you. We love you. We worry about you. We want to bring you back to us. Stephen . . . you are going to have to stop living in that club, take what little money you have left with you and invest it in your own future. Before it is too late! It that clear enough?"

"Perfectly."

"Well?"

I felt my damage control defenses crumbling away. I knew that if I started crying I was done for: I knew that I had to hang on and weather the storm. In any case it really was time for me to talk about my parents. I never did talk about my parents save for giving the bare bones details of their business and their accident with anyone including myself. I had simply blocked all that out. Let's see, what did people want to hear? They wanted me to admit that I felt horrible and that I was scared to death. At that moment I could have used Jeremy Lighter's imagination. It would have been nice for my real self to be taken along for a ride while my less-than-real self was engaged in short-term therapy, or was it acting? It would have been nice to be nothing more than a witness to my own suffering. But I had no such talents. Jeremy was the poet with the vivid imagination and the fancy theories; I was only an idler with a small bag of tricks. I started speaking and my voice sounded as if it was coming from nowhere. Would it stop on the surface of my body or would it go flying off into the atmosphere? It was coming on at full speed, from out of nowhere, and it was exploding apart who I was, but for whom? I was only dimly aware, now, that this baring of my soul was just what my friends were expecting of me. Even so, I plunged straight ahead knowing there was just the slightest chance that I was really faking all this emotion and doing so only to make the trio staring at me over the dinner table feel successful. I looked from face to face, and said, dramatically:

"House and home. My parents really had no way of making that fundamental human distinction. In fact, the Lattimore family has had that problem since Colonial days. My ancestors grabbed all the land they could and then certain members went off to live in clubs. My parents and I were no different. My parents sold real estate, our own houses included. I think they bought, improved and sold for profit no less than nine houses we lived in before I got to the eighth grade. As well, they bought and sold condominiums, ranch houses, and colonial houses, and of course lots and lots of these raised ranches. My parents sold whole tracts of them, the way that guy we visited this morning sells cider. Line them up and sell them to the folks!

"Now I know that a person's selling real estate has nothing to do with that same person's not being able to distinguish between a house and a home. I know that. But my parents were unlike other people who sold real estate. They were lacking in certain fundamentals. To cover up that lack, they developed, instead, a real disdain for holding on to what they called "square footage." Houses were just shifting segments of controlled space for them. Living . . . in space and time . . . was a temporary situation thrust upon my parents, one that made them uncomfortable and one that embarrassed them. They sold houses as a means of *confessing* their sins of occupancy. They sold houses in order to do penance for being alive *here* as opposed to being in some transcendent *there*. They might have been *thrown* into space and time but they took the blame for it anyway.

"My parents were deeply religious people. No one knew how deeply religious they were besides me. They did not go to any church . . . I can't say they were Christians in any sense . . . they were more like the ancient Gnostics. That is, they really hated the world. They thought the world was an evil place and that they were trapped within it. They figured, rightly or wrongly, that the only way they could get free of the evil world was to sell it off, to sell the very places in which they dwelled. They figured that if they had time to buy and then to sell the *whole* world they could finally escape it for good. Of course, their plan did not work. It was as if they were running in place while sinking into quicksand at the same time. They could sell off portions of space, but not their living place in the world. Worse, when the real estate market was slowed down, they felt personally responsible for their own depleted economic condition. Money did not make them feel condemned, property did. They were strangers to the universe because they dwelled in the universe. Of course, they didn't go about *preaching* this point of view, I really only read this into their behavior myself. You might say that while my parents were given over to bouts of depression, I only had a theory about why they were so sad.

"I never did give in to the way my parents thought, at least not completely. I never had serious trouble with bouts of depression nor with overwhelming feelings of guilt. Yet I know how to deal with people who do. That is because I have been brought up to do so. I am like a man who grew up sighted but whose parents were both born blind. Such a man can deal with blind people. I can deal with people driven by irrational guilt.

"True, I did not escape that tragedy down in Virginia without suffering terrible damage to my own psyche. I admit it. I admit, as well, that I can never look at a house, at any ordinary house and not think of it as a commodity to be sold for profit. I cannot simply dwell *anywhere* on the earth but I can dwell . . . shall we say . . . selectively. I have to! I am not religious the way my parents were. So, rather than my agreeing with you that I ought to be living your life style, that I ought to be *returning* to it, I can tell you that I never have lived that way and do not think I ever can live that way. So, I live in one room. Living in one room gives me the illusion that I am surrounded by some sort of invisible barrier."

Josh had heard enough. He shouted:

"You're going broke!"

"I don't care!"

Jane, the only one at the table who did not know me and had never met me before this day, put a wry if toothy smile on her face. She was sitting back in her Queen Anne style-dining chair and she eyed me with amused suspicion. Still smiling at me, she placed one hand on Judy's arm and said:

"I think your boyfriend is pulling our legs. I have no idea why."

At once all those feelings that were welling up either for me or for the others, I was still not sure which, for I could as well move myself to tears as I could someone else, were gone and I burst out laughing. Josh shook his head and then even he gave a laugh. He did not want to, his kept his lips sealed, but the laugh came rushing out his nostrils. There was still the terrible fact of my going broke to be dealt with, but this now seemed to take second place behind my lingering uncertainty about what? No doubt Josh believed I was now acting out of arrogance. Only Judy still looked hurt and concerned. I turned to her and tried to present her as sincere a look as one human being can present to another. This was the woman who loved me and was willing to spend the rest of her life with me, however long that might be.

"Judy? "I asked. "What do you think?"

"I suggest that you leave the Medallion Club and come live with me at my place in Hempstead. The rent on my apartment is only five hundred dollars a month. I suggest that you let Josh and Jane take over your remaining finances and put you on some sort of controlled stipend or allowance. I suggest that you consult with them on how to invest the rest of the money you got from your parents business in . . . ah. . . ."

She finally faltered. Very softly, I asked:

"In what?"

Judy looked at Jane, who nodded affirmatively. Obviously the three of them had talked every detail of my future over in advance. Judy went on, though her voice was growing fainter.

"You could go to law school like Josh did. You could go to school nights while working with me, days."

"I see. Invest what remains of my money in more schooling. That's one idea. What else?"

Judy looked over at Josh this time. He did not nod affirmatively. He only lifted his eyebrows in a rather non-committal way. My guess was that what I had just said about my parents, whether anyone believed me or not, was constraining Judy here. She took a deep breath and said what she had to say anyway.

"Well. I mean. . . . I studied management in college? I know about business. You grew up learning about your parent's business. Josh told me that it was your intent to go into the family business when you graduated from college. He said that the only reason you did not get into that business right away was because of a certain downturn that happened right as you were graduating. But while you lived at home, Stephen, and you *did* live at home and not just in some house about to be rolled over for a profit, you certainly were boning up on the business. All businesses have down cycles, right? That is no reason not to be in them. All we do during a downturn is, you know, like . . . tighten our belts. It takes years, sometimes, to get a business off the ground and to make it secure. That is what I want to do, Stephen. I love you. I want to go into business with you. I want you to live with me and I want you to put your money into buying property out on the island. Law school or no law school, you know about property. Now is a good time to start putting your knowledge into practice. I'm not saying you'll end up like Donald Trump or anything but . . . you know . . . you are really smart, Stephen. You could be like The Donald."

I gazed over at my precious Judy. How could I not love a woman who saw that much potential in me? She could be the one to save me at that. As well, there was nothing like the prospect of making a fat profit in business while clinging to one's millstone scruples, too. Though it would be a long, long battle fighting my way up from a five hundred dollar a month apartment in Hempstead to being a real estate player in Manhattan. Whoops. Make that a player out on the island, for there just wasn't enough room in the city for both The Donald and me.

"I'll think it over, folks," I said dryly.

We spent another hour or so at Josh and Jane's and then they drove us back to the station in Hartford where we got on another train back to the city. It wasn't so crowded going back. Judy and I said little or nothing to one another; we held hands and Judy fell asleep with her head on my shoulder. I put my arm around her and with my other hand I inadvertently patted my wallet. It occurred to me that if someone has money, real money, they don't even have to bother being polite to people. If they are polite, they only do so voluntarily. I had been that way for five years running. I was mostly polite to people out of kindness but I did not have to act that way. I did not have to please a boss or have to lobby anyone for favors or beg people I knew or did not know for some sort of place in this world. I had less than three years left to spend my parent's money. I had two more things for sure: I had my scruples and I had possession of Jeremy Lighter's winning lottery ticket. Those were the two considerations driving me back then. They were what could either save me or curse me.

Chapter Ten

As soon as I got back to New York I called Jeremy Lighter and he and I agreed to share a dinner on the following Monday at the rooftop dining room at the Medallion Club. He gave no reason for his lingering on in the city after the holiday though I had a pretty good idea what was taking place. We were both eager to bring closure to what ever it was we had festering between us, though neither one of us could or would say *what* that was, if it was anything. Were we friends or enemies? Did we know one another's secrets or were we only pretending to do so? One thing for sure, we were able to communicate aesthetically.

We were given a table by a window and sat facing one another over a gleaming, white, starched tablecloth. We both wore dark suits. We dealt with menu decisions swiftly. Jeremy ordered wild mushroom bisque en crute, seafood Navarn with lobster sauce, a spinach salad *sans* the sliced mushrooms offered, tournedos of veal and beef *sans* the grilled eggplant offered, a slice of chocolate velvet cake and regular coffee. I ordered penne pasta with proscuitto, smoked salmon with virgin olive oil substituted for the offered mustard dill sauce, a plate of mixed garden greens *sans* the offered addition of red cabbage, roast leg of lamb substituting apple sauce for the usual mint jelly, raspberry mousse in a chocolate cup and regular tea. The wines selection did slow us down a bit; we finally settled on one bottle of Northern Californian dry Riesling for Jeremy and a bottle of Sangiovese from Terme, Italy, for me, along with two glasses of red Doubonnet with vodka, over ice, to start our meal.

Now that Thanksgiving was over the festive atmosphere of the Christmas season was pervading the club; all the private dining rooms were spoken for and at the rooftop dining room it was difficult to get reservations. Judy actually had to pull some strings to get us seated where we were. It was most gracious of her to do that as a favor to me. When the vodka-laced glasses of Dubonnet arrived we toasted one another effusively, but we spoke very little as the meal unfolded. That was the way with Jeremy and me; we liked to hold our fire until most of the dishes were cleared away from our unannounced but still formal battle field. It was only when I was dipping my spoon into the last of my mousse that an odd idea struck me. First, I patted my breast pocket to make sure a certain piece of paper was still there; I even turned my eyes to his breast pocket to see if it was bulging. It was. This was my idea. I would adopt a bantering tone with the poet, then I would reach into the breast pocket of my suit, pull out my wallet, open it up, pull out the folded lottery ticket and lay it out on the white tablecloth between us and say:

"Oh by the bye, Jeremy, old boy, this is yours. The winner. Go ahead, man! Pick it up! It's worth thirty seven million dollars."

I swear, I *could* imagine myself doing and saying all that at some time. It was just that I could not imagine my doing it *then and there*. I had an Augustinian streak in me as well. As I hesitated, a wide grin frozen on my face, Jeremy boomed out:

"We always seem to start our serious discussions but harking back to childhood, Stephen. *My* childhood. I suppose we should end there, too. Is that all right with you?"

The grin disappeared from my face and my hand stopped patting my breast pocket.

"I wouldn't have it any other way, Jeremy."

"I went once, as a child, into another neighbor's yard. They lived on the other side of us, on the side away from where lived the boy and his toys."

"I got it."

"They built a children's swing set. It was an ordinary contraption with two steel bars converging on one side and another two steel bars converging on the other side and with a steel cross bar connecting both. Two swings hung from this cross bar."

"I think I know what a swing set looks like, Jeremy."

"I'm sorry. I was only picturing. . . ."

"Go on. Go on."

The waiter came to see if we needed anything else. We did not, but then again we were not inclined to move, either. So we ordered cognac. With cognac, we could hold our glasses in our hands, swirl the liquid about, study its color, sniff its aroma and otherwise take our time consuming it while Jeremy got on with what he said was to be his final tale. He proceeded at last, once again darting his flint-blue eyes in my direction at the most unexpected moments.

"Now, Stephen, let us be clear about this. The last time I told you of an adventure I had when leaving my yard, I used what we might call mystical terms or metaphysical terms or spiritual terms or whatever. You did not seem sympathetic or even comfortable with this language. I suspect you want modern explanations for my actions. That is fine with me. Yet modern terms can be just as esoteric as are the old ones, if you think about it."

"Esoteric?"

"Yes. Only in the modern sense, the whole world digests the same terminology and doesn't realize that what they are digesting remains a theory and a secretive one at that. The truth stays hidden from us. But who am I to insist on a classical approach to these painful experiences. Let us say, then, that my irrational *id* was tweaked. Is tweaked a good action word? Would Freud approve? I say to hell with him. We will use his terms and leave him out of it. Let us say that my id tugged at me. Let us say that I had an overwhelming desire to swing on the neighbor's swings. I left the yard."

"Under another dark at day?"

"No. I only saw the dark at day once."

"So you went to the neighbor's yard on the opposite side of you."

"I did."

"And you used their swing set."

"I did. I swung on the one on my right first, then on the one on my left."

"And you suffered guilt because of that."

"Not at all. I felt entitled to swing on those swings. That is a contemporary sin, Stephen. Feeling entitled to something. But as I child I could not grasp such a nicety."

"What happened then? Why are you telling me this story?"

"I am telling you because . . . while I was swinging on the left swing the swing set broke."

"The chain broke?"

"No. One of the converging bars on the left side of the set became detached and the whole swing set sagged."

"That doesn't sound like much to worry about."

"You wouldn't think so. Nevertheless, I was plunged into a terrible state of guilt."

"I thought you could bear guilt, Jeremy, because you could convert it to beauty."

"Not this time. This time the *quality* of my quilt was unbearably heavy. I had never felt anything like it before. It wasn't possible for me to convert it to anything aesthetic. It was . . . I suppose you could call it . . . pathological. The urgings of my id were gone; I was now in the grip of my super ego."

"Tell me something. Had your Dad told you the story of his stolen cigarettes yet?"

"Yes, he . . . he had just done so."

"I see."

The cognac arrived. We played with it.

"In any case, the guilt I felt was unprecedented. I could not bear the discomfort."

"Was it worse than shame? You said, about shame, that . . ."

"I know what I said about shame. Shame is more intense than ordinary guilt. What I had seemed of a different scale."

"You said 'pathological.'"

"That's right. My life seemed to disintegrate right in front of me. I knew that I would keep giving in to what you called temptations and that it would render me helplessly guilty in some abnormal way."

"What did you do about it?"

"I told my Dad."

We both laughed. We clicked cognac glasses and sipped. I felt on safer ground with Jeremy that moment. And yet a moment later he was staring hard at me with those flint-blue eyes of his. I turned my own eyes to my cognac glass. I said nothing and waited for him to continue. He did so but only after taking a very long pause. My cheeks were burning.

"I thought Dad would be impressed, seeing how he was so tortured. He was not. He seemed bored with my story. It was such a little story after all."

"What did he suggest you do about it?"

"He had me wait in the house while he went over to assess the damage. When he came back, he tried being clever. I suppose he was trying to keep me from living in the same kind of moral hell he was suffering. He said: 'You cannot really say you *broke* the swing set; it was only that you happened to be on one of the swings when the swing set did break!' You see he was trying to help me."

"Go on."

"He asked me to tell him *precisely* what happened to the swing set to cause it to sag on me. I said that one of the pipes became detached. It sounded so damn silly once I said it! That was all that had happened. A pipe came out of its fitting. They have . . . there was this fitting in each corner. It had three holes, two for the bars that came up from the ground to meet at this fitting, a third to hold the cross bar. Anyway, I finally admitted, to Dad and to myself, that the swing set was not utterly destroyed. Why, it could be fixed quite easily! Dad asked me suddenly:

"How much do you think it would cost to repair that swing set so it is as good as new?"

"What did you tell him?"

"Five dollars."

I had to laugh. As I laughed, the words "five dollars" came out of my mouth in two noisy puffs. Even Jeremy joined me in laughter.

"That is the only dollar figure I could think of at the moment."

"Did your Dad agree with your estimate?"

"He did. Then he . . . I suppose he was just being my Dad but . . . he made a practical suggestion. He offered me a way out."

"Makes sense."

"You think it made sense, Stephen?"

"Well. I do. That is . . . well I think your father was trying to help you if all you required was having your sense of justice fulfilled according to your own idea of your own deserts. You said yourself that he was being pathological about those cigarettes. He did not want you to go down the same tortured path. But I can hardly blame him for that."

"I did not blame Dad for anything!"

"OK. Don't get excited, Jeremy. Remember where we are. And remember that we are talking about childhood. Remember that we are talking about a five dollar repair job."

"Yes. Dad and I talked about my allowance. I was given ten cents a day for an allowance. Dad suggested I save, half of it, five cents a day, for one hundred days and then give the five dollars either to the people who owned the swing set . . . I could do it anonymously by dropping it in the mail . . . or else I could give the five dollars over to some charity. He recommended I give it to the local Lion's Club, saying something about blind people."

"Well? Did you do what he said?"

"No."

"Why?"

"I'll tell you. My ego was born on the spot. I thrust all other considerations aside. I was being *me*. I was only concerned with me, alone."

"So, you are like your father, after all. You have to have your little, suffering, pathological self. What did you say to your father?"

"I told him, as much to my own surprise as his, that it would be a cold day in hell before I would turn half my allowance over to my grimy neighbors or to the blind, or to anyone!"

"What did your father say to that?"

"He realized that the story he told me, about the cigarettes, had hurt me more than either of us could fathom. He realized that my ego was born *on top of* my sense of guilt. And there was nothing he could do about it. There was nothing I could do about it. We were both doomed. The only difference between us was that I was going to become a poet."

I held my tongue. No doubt this was serious business. This was no snickering child's tale for sure. I played with my glass until Jeremy was able to continue.

"Now I am a poet. I have an ego and yet I suffer enormous amounts of guilt and shame. I carry the evil one inside me permanently."

He looked at me. I saw hell in his eyes. I thought: hell is blue.

"Look, Jeremy, I . . . these childhood things are. . . ."

"Don't say it. Don't try to minimize the feelings that have shaped me. My own ego was born *above* the ground of my personal hell and that damned me forever. That is what the ancient teaching is all about, is it not? We are born out of a desire to be ourselves and we are condemned for that."

Our eyes were locked together. I got just a slight taste of what he was suffering. I was overwhelmed. Jeremy's flint-blue eyes filled with tears. I thought these tears would begin steaming as they fell on his cheeks.

"If you are going to be any good as a writer then you must suffer as I do, Stephen."

"I . . . see."

I was not sure if I saw anything, really. After all, what exactly had I heard coming out of this man's mouth? I heard only trivial tales of childhood along with a couple of late-adolescent misunderstandings. Could a man be reduced to tears because he failed to make a single introduction at a garden party, or because he spoke up to his father? Surely Jeremy was only using incidents from childhood in order to foster his artistic sensitivity. It was too much! Then again, the look in that man's eyes was enough to condemn both of us!

I compared Jeremy's words to me with my performance at the Thanksgiving dinner up at Josh and Jane's house. I wondered: was this man being honest with me or was he merely using me as a sounding board for ideas strained through his long-gone child's mind?

"Jeremy!" I began rather sternly. "I don't . . . listen. What you do as a poet quite obviously requires an enormous emotional and intellectual and aesthetic commitment on your part. You live without any defenses in place. But can't you step aside from all that now and then? I have seen you smile. I have heard you laugh. You yourself told me how much fun you have with your poetry group . . . the ones who refuse to be your critics? Surely you have ah . . . on top of everything else . . . a mundane existence that allows you to relax, don't you?"

"Do you think that sort of thing helps me?"

"Well . . . you tell me."

He gave me what I considered to be a sick look. He said:

"You know all about me now, Stephen. You are the only person on this earth who knows all about me. I have given you my ideas, my theories, my insights. In fact I have given you *everything* I have or can have. Don't try to deny it. I have drawn you into my horror despite everything. I cannot shift my *pain* away from me and onto you but I can and I think I have let you know what is behind my pain. Have I not done so? Have I not given you what I have?"

"You have."

"Then do not belittle me by appealing to my mundane existence."

"I'm sorry."

Jeremy shook his head and then he looked at me with disappointment and disgust in his eyes.

"I am telling you about the soul of a poet, Stephen. I am telling you about suffering. Do not disappoint me at this stage of the game."

He said this and then he just looked at me. I had to tell him something.

"Please, Jeremy. I plead with you. Have the courage to bear what you have to bear. Or, failing that, do take what is yours. Please do. That is to say . . . just ask! You can have whatever is coming to you. I swear."

"What are you saying to me? Do you have something to offer me?"

"Perhaps I do."

"Do you? Is there anything you wish to give me?"

I looked at him and I said:

"Here! All right. Here."

I stood up and reached for my wallet but Jeremy jumped up a moment later, jumped up with a great, almost desperate burst of energy and he held his arm out at me, as if he was a traffic cop telling me to stop. His voice boomed out all over the rooftop dining room:

"Forget it! Forget it, Stephen. I have tried explaining myself to you. Just . . . just leave me alone now, will you? It's too late. It is just too late."

He walked away. I stood by the table. The waiters came rushing over to be solicitous, to quiet down a possible scene, to be on hand or whatever. I assured them that all was well and after giving Jeremy a few minute lead I took the elevator down to the eighth floor and went to my room. I did not know what to think anymore. I didn't know what to do. I *still* insisted that I was a man with scruples who would do what was right and necessary, when the time came.

Chapter Eleven

Came midnight Christmas Eve at the Medallion Club. It had been quiet in the building for days. There was only a skeletal staff on duty; all the frenetic activities of the season ended the Friday before and would not pick up again until the following weekend. I did not attend any of the holiday festivities myself; then again I rarely did. I still don't. I always thought of the club as my dwelling place, not my activities center.

I was seated at my desk again, trying to sort out what had happened and all that had not yet happened to those of us who were caught up in this "incident" as I finally came to call it. I had grown impatient. I wanted to deal with the matter of the lottery ticket at last. I wanted to speak plainly. Yet there I was again, starting off in my usual, oblique way, by offering what could only be a labeled a scattered presentation of thoughts plucked right off the top of my head then allowed to float down onto the paper like so many invisible snowflakes. Was I incorrigible? I swear I was still being honest. In any case, I knew that all would be settled soon enough.

What were the facts? Jeremy Lighter, who lingered on in room 806 on a daily basis, having taken a leave of absence from his school I presume, and who took to glaring at me with his awful blue eyes while not speaking to me through his cutting tool lips whenever we crossed paths either in the hallway or on the elevator, had, weeks earlier delivered unto me what he thought constituted *a* theory of aesthetics. I had already critiqued his main ideas. I had also read his poetry. Despite my unfamiliarity with poetry I believed that I understood his theory and found it wanting in certain respects. Yet Jeremy was a successful poet. Therefore I concluded that his aesthetic talents, his command of language, had no direct connection with his heightened sense of perception. He was a conventional poet after all. Yet if this is true then everything Jeremy said to me over these last few weeks was of no relevance whatsoever, at least not in reference to him as a professional poet. Then again I might have been wrong; what he told me might have been of the utmost importance in all phases of his life.

I could only offer the unsupported judgment that Jeremy's extraordinary perceptual talents were wrongheaded in some fundamental respect. His theory was perhaps coherent but it lacked anything like correspondence with the known laws of what?

Physics, I feared. Jeremy must have taken seriously, or much too seriously, this metaphor of light, or this so-called perceptual and intellectual illumination that so dominated metaphysical thinking until the Nineteenth Century. Once more, I do not think he ever did sort out the distinction between light as a medium that allows one to see, and seeing itself, be it sensual or intellectual. I suppose he could, while clinging to something that was cohesive even if it led him into error when he tried to literally see what is illuminated, still manage to make himself into a successful poet regardless: who the hell was going to check up on him, anyway? Who the hell would deny that what Jeremy Lighter kept inside himself with Cartesian strictness, or projected outside himself in some utterly strange way, worked in print? Ptolemy, to use one example from a long list of successful but misguided people, had it all wrong about the cosmos but that didn't prevent him from enjoying one whale of a career in astronomy at that.

Jeremy's ideas on aesthetics were perhaps better approached as being ideas of the imagination exploited pragmatically. They worked for him but they landed him in trouble with people like me, people, and here I am not bragging but merely being honest, who had a better handle on the employment of these ideas-in-use. To quote the words I wrote it in my notebook back then:

"Jeremy's use of his creative imagination in the guise of poetry is like a scientist of yesteryear making use of the caloric theory of heat. Jeremy can keep on raising the temperature, so to speak, but he cannot ascribe these applications within any known limit. Theoretically, his imagination has no limit and that is his flaw.

"On the other hand, my theory of idleness as being our most enlightened state is like the modern, molecular theory of heat. My idleness hovers comfortably above absolute zero and in a constant state; I do know my limits and I never exceed them. I never get too caught up in things like guilt or shame. True, I do have my millstone scruples, but surely there is a difference between having scruples and having an inner life that causes you to be unhappy, unstable and ultimately unhinged!

"That difference is easy to spell out. Anyone who champions Jeremy's way of life depends upon the whim of the creative imagination while I am first and foremost a man of principle. I do not have to imagine, remember, think or exercise will power in order to be; all I have to do is to adhere to the principle of idleness. I stay idle for as long as I can and I don't bother my head about it. I have already explained *ad nauseam* that I deny that boredom is part of the *human* condition. That is not to say that individual human beings cannot be or are not in fact often bored. But they ought to get over it! It is just their way of making excuses for getting mixed up in such things as thirty-year mortgages, investment wars, and corporate takeovers. What I think is that people do not hurl themselves into higher and higher levels of commitment because they would be bored otherwise; they are dissatisfied with what thrills them and so they come to the outrageous conclusion that boredom is inescapable. There really is no such thing, condition, mood, emotion or process called boredom that is of any *philosophical* interest. It takes years of concentrated idleness to realize that great truth.

"Oh, we can and we sometimes do change our essential description of ourselves depending upon how we go forth to meet one, two or all three of those worlds Jeremy mentioned to me, including the environment, the Other and one's own ego, but these changes we do make prove inauthentic when all is said and done. Truth be told, I do not really believe that I exist, or that others exist or that the world exists in any authentic way. What is authentic is your knowing that it is just those moments of contemplation we enjoy when we are completely idle. What counts is that we *are* idle. Of course we are mortal, too, but what can we do about that?

"Idleness remains our highest goal despite our terrible limitation of time or temperature. Furthermore, it is perfectly all right for us to chase after the fulfillment of our necessary carnal needs while we are maintaining a state of idleness. Everyone does so whether they want to admit it or not. It is the ascetics who are the big hypocrites in this regard. I ask you, why eat only one measly bowl of gruel every other day if you have to eat, regardless? Better to eat a burger with French fries at the Medallion Club every day for lunch, and then look forward to a good dinner, too!

"What are my millstone scruples, then? They are nothing more, at bottom, than the practice of good manners.

"Much of what happened has to be considered Jeremy's fault, I must say. His inner life has taken so long to unfold.

"Once more, it is the case that Jeremy's inner life is too rich! It is filled with storms rather than calm, it is a weight to bear rather than an uplifting help; it is a childish obsession rather than a maturing growth and, at bottom I feel I am the stronger one because I am leaner down in my soul. Mine is not the supererogatory call to ethical sacrifice regardless of whether or not this ethical call is transformed into something aesthetic or not, nor is mine the hypersensitive turning to some sort of conscious perception of greater reality. I never claimed I was more a creature of nature than Jeremy Lighter. I never claimed that Jeremy Lighter is more of a transcendent being than me. I do not even wish to take too much credit for holding to the opposite view of our respective roles. All I am saying is that I can handle certain unspecified responsibilities with aplomb whereas Jeremy cannot even get along with himself despite his having a critic-free group of friends to ease his passage through life. His father was a non-critic; but only after he poisoned his son with guilt. These shortcomings do make a difference.

"I was not born rich. My parents labored away despite their distrust and dislike of this world of private property. I am their flesh and blood but I am my grandfather's issue. Thus it is that I do not and will not stoop to labor. I contemplate. I do only what suffices. I know that none of us live forever. All I ask is that I be allowed to attain to my own base of necessity, though for how long I still am not prepared to say. This is the initial condition. The condition must be met. Life is not worth living otherwise. That, and the fact that I am dispassionate I count among my greatest strengths.

"There are others in this world like me. There always have been others like me. There was my grandfather, and there is that mean old man who makes me wait for Great-grandfather's suite. We belong to the contemplative set; we live on this earth without boredom. That is the truth. Once more, I suspect that our numbers are growing! This growing number of souls harboring a burning ambition to live the good life for man just does not fit into the static contours of eternal contemplation, the very task we are to perform in our idleness. This is to say that even as the numbers of idle human beings grows, only a few of us have the knack to be properly idle. We have to draw the line somewhere. Jeremy was right about our being *in the way* of one another. It is worse among the idle.

"Jeremy simply does not want to see himself as he really is. He imagines himself dwelling outside his own being. He does not look in the mirror in order to grab a visible image of himself that he can then identify with, calling that glimpsed bodily image his ego. No. Jeremy performs a little trick of his own, one that solves everything and nothing. Jeremy removes himself to a location that even he cannot see into or out of, so that he may keep the sinner in him a stranger. Jeremy is weighted down with too many considerations. Jeremy is a victim of his own literary talent."

Looking back on those words I wrote then, I cannot help but cheer. I was right then and I am right now. But there were other considerations pressing me as the Christmas holiday was upon us and the cold days of winter settled into the northeast. Judy Knoffer's desire to marry me was stronger than ever, and her intention of turning me into a middle-class clone was still a frightening possibility. Judy, backed up by a meddling Jane and Josh, were becoming, shall I say, a *destabilizing* force in my life. Judy was increasing her influence over me from daily! She had been keeping it up since Thanksgiving. She was confident she could eventually outflank me and then swallow me up. Thanks to Judy I had begun making trips out to the island nights and weekends. What did we do when we got there? We went both house and home hunting!

Judy had her eye on this one semi-detached brick house and home located on a cul-de-sac in Elmont, one that was only three minutes from some highway or other. Before she took me out to look at it she explained:

"We can get it for around three hundred thousand, Stephen. Really. It's a steal. It has a mother-in-law apartment built into the rear; the family who owns this house extended the basement out into the rear yard and incorporated this second unit into the overall scheme. You can't make changes like that anymore on that street so this house I am telling you about is a real bargain. We can rent that second unit out. Stephen? This will work!"

I remember the taxi ride out to this house Judy wanted us to buy. I remember the Christmas lights on the houses we passed. I remember the plastic Santa Clauses and the plywood reindeer and the wire mesh angels and the miles and miles of winking, blinking colored light bulbs. In a way I do think this was something like Jeremy was trying to capture in his theory of seeing; Jeremy was just trying to see all the pretty lights.

Anyway, the house Judy had her eye on, the one we looked at, was a low, brick building on a street of low, brick buildings.

I thought: What the hell am I doing here? Judy said:

"It comes with a washer and dryer but we'll have to change them; I am not going to put up with front loaders. What do you think?"

"Definitely not. We'll have to get top loaders."

Judy liked to hear things like that. For my part, I just let the words roll off my lips.

Judy said she liked the drapes the seller was leaving behind. This house had insulated drapes strung out across the entire length of one wall in the living room. You would never know there was a window behind them; they were thicker than a stage curtain.

"I like the size, Stephen. And I like the idea of blocking out the highway noise. What do you think of the color?"

"Well, isn't sky blue better to be seen up there in the sky rather than standing up across the vertical horizon of your living room?"

"Our living room, darling. And don't be silly. Sky blue is a light color. It makes the room look spacey. Like outside."

"Sorry."

The owners of this place had filled entire rooms with oversized furniture that was still encased in plastic covers. They were willing to sell entire rooms of this furniture to us. Judy was willing to listen to them. She whispered to me before these negotiations began:

"If they think I am going to buy that dining set into the bargain they have another thought coming."

I was more alarmed regarding the encased Spanish couches. I tried to intervene at one point in the furniture negotiations, telling Judy that I wanted none of it, but she showed herself to be patient with me. She knew my weaknesses despite my experience in certain matters to do with real estate; she was determined to take the lead in any case.

"If we get this mortgage we won't have a lot of money left over for revovations, and the bathroom needs to be completely redone except for the tiles around the sink. So, I think that if we get a bargain on the furniture we will be ahead of the game until your business gets going? Stephen? You do see what I mean, don't you?"

"Right."

While plans for us to purchase our starter house and home went forward with lightning speed, we were also looking into the real estate business I was to begin out here on the cusp of Queens. The idea, vaguely introduced during the Thanksgiving dinner I had attended in Connecticut but now honed to greater perfection by Judy herself, was for me to put half my remaining cash into some stocks that Josh and Jane were following. As for the balance of my money: I was to invest all of it into what amounted to ten percent down on two contiguous row houses located some ten blocks or so from the house we were looking to buy for ourselves. Judy saw this last move quite clearly.

"You buy them, you paint them up inside and then you turn around and sell them. Law school will have to be put on hold; you are going to be busy, nights, sprucing up our investments. People are flooding this area, Stephen. You know they are. All you have to do is keep one jump ahead of the horde. You know what to do, darling. Buy, paint, and then sell. You can not miss!"

She was right, of course. I knew she was right because her declarative sentences no longer ended in rising–voice question marks when she spoke. I mumbled something, and then, just to change the subject, said:

"Josh and Jane are not going to get married until next April. What are they waiting for?"

"What is wrong with waiting? I think we should wait until after the summer, ourselves. House and home first, I say. Don't you agree?"

"Certainly."

"I mean, one is better off moving into a nest, not trying to build it after the honeymoon."

"You've got that right."

After an uncomfortable pause, Judy came right out and asked:

"Stephen, why are you still at the club? Think of the drain on your finances. Why don't you move in with me now?"

I did not have a roll-off-the-tongue answer for this one, so I played the old reluctant male role.

"You have to give a guy a few weeks to get used to things, Judy."

"What things?"

"Things that are . . . moving so fast."

Speed did not seem to bother Judy. In fact, Judy was quitting the Medallion Club at the end of the year to take a job in hotel management out at Kennedy Airport.

"There is money in thinking about the comfort of the international traveler," she explained.

Judy liked the idea of not having to go into the city and fight all that congestion. Of course the airport hotel was not exactly located in the country but I was told she could get in and out of there and back to either Elmont or Hempstead in good time.

"They have a shuttle for us. And there are these back roads. We get right in. It's not like we are going to be like airline passengers or anything. Besides, we will be moving soon."

"Ah."

Despite all these plans I still hesitated to withdraw my money from the bank that was paying me so little interest that it was as good as no interest at all. Living off one's principal is so convenient, after all. I must have looked, to Judy, like a man daydreaming on the railroad tracks. His dreams might be sweet, but . . . ! Finally, Judy called for a showdown.

"Stephen! Are you going to leave the Medallion Club or are you not?"

"I tell you what, darling. Let me stay on through January at the club. What do you say?"

"You don't have to stay another day in that club, Stephen. Josh and Jane want us to come back up to Connecticut between Christmas and New Year. To help us shore up our plans. What do you say?"

"Oh. Jane! And Josh! I'll tell you what. Just give me a few days to wrap up my thoughts. Old habits, you know."

"I will tell you one thing, Mr. Lattimore, you are not going to go on staying up all night and then napping afternoons. That is over! You are going to have to be up and out, serving your customers, once we launch this business. I'll help when I am not on duty out at the airport."

"Thank you."

Judy sent me back to the club with instructions to "wrap up" my writing about a gentleman of leisure, right my sleep habits, and then meet her in the lobby of the club at noon on Christmas Day.

"I will be in the lobby Christmas Day at noon and you had better be downstairs with the final bill from the Medallion Club in your hands. You hear me?"

I will never forget her tone of voice as she said that. That was the voice of middle-class authority. The middle class does not call out to us like a god from above, it dictates to us at eye level.

I wrote through the night, Christmas Eve. I got up at ten a.m., as usual, and took a leisurely shower. Then I went back to bed. I was going to stay in bed until just before noon, and then wander down to the lobby and make excuses to Judy, stall her, whatever, but things did not work out quite the way I planned. Or, maybe they did. These are the trials of existence we can never be sure of; these are the interesting moments of life.

I was lying in bed at eleven a.m. Christmas morning when Judy, who arrived at the club an hour early, let herself in with her passkey. I had failed to put on the chain lock. Judy caught Adele and me lying there, stark naked and playing a little game with the maid's vacuum cleaner hose. I will not insult the sensibilities of the reader by explaining the rules of this game, nor will I bother to explain what Adele was doing in my room on Christmas morning.

While Adele was willing to get down on the carpet and have it out, physically, with Judy, I must say Judy maintained her dignity despite her shock. Of course, getting caught lying naked in bed with the maid meant an end to Judy's plans for my future out on the island. Gone were plans for the purchase of that semi-detached house and home with the last of its kind, mother-in-law, income producing unit; gone was the chance to buy two contiguous row houses along with the opportunity to paint them and turn them over for profit, and gone were plans for a late summer wedding. My invitation to Josh and Jane's wedding would be withdrawn as well. I was being denied both Elmont and West Simsbury. How awful.

Judy never came back to the club and I never saw her again. Adele left, too. Turns out she had a sister in the Dominican Republic. I told her she didn't have to move there. I told her that none of the screaming and yelling that took place between Judy and me really had anything to do with her. Never mind what she said to me in return. Suffice to say both women stormed out of the Medallion Club that day. As for me, I went to lunch and then took my afternoon nap. I am a man of steady habits.

When I woke up at six that evening I knew what had to be done. I had made up my mind. Believe it or not, I still had my scruples. In short, I decided to turn the winning ticket over to Jeremy Lighter at long last. I decided to place the thirty seven million dollars in the hands of its rightful owner. That decision was the one I was going to make all along. Believe me. I know that ought implies can.

I called Jeremy up on the telephone. He was in his room and he answered at once.

"Hello?"

His voice sounded hollow.

"Jeremy"

"Stephen. Yes. What do you want?"

"I have something that belongs to you. I take it you will be leaving here soon. I want to get this to you before you go."

Once again there was a longish pause on the telephone. I could hear the man's labored breathing. Had he been sleeping, too? He said:

"Time is it?"

"Six"

"Ah. Six. Tell you what. Give me until tomorrow. Will you do that, Stephen? Will you give me until eleven tomorrow morning?"

"All right. Till then."

"Good bye."

It was an odd request Jeremy was making. Why put it off now? Didn't he know what I was bringing to him? I still was not sure.

I went out into the city, looking for a place to have dinner. It was bitter cold out and so I ducked into the nearby Algonquin. It occurred to me that Jeremy might try to flee the club overnight without seeing me. It wouldn't do him any good. I would just look him up down in Virginia and hand him the ticket anyway. I would show up in the school where he taught eighth grade math. I would burst into his classroom, waving the ticket before the startled eyes of all those youngsters, shouting:

"Yo! Jeremy! Look! You are rich!"

I recognized my limitations more clearly than ever before. Idleness had not corrupted me. On the contrary, idleness had saved me. Two years from now, I thought, I will be . . . I still drew a blank when I tried looking ahead. I was no better off than all the great thinkers in this regard; I could not stick the passage of time into timeless eternity. I did not care. I had been happy. I would not spoil my happiness by being greedy. So you see, it is not that I was tempted to steal Jeremy's lottery ticket, it was just that, having my mind ever focused upon higher things, I felt it was all right to wait a while before returning it.

I ordered a five-course meal and two bottles of wine. Then I sat in the hotel lounge drinking cognac. I didn't leave the Algonquin until midnight. When I got back the Medallion Club I was both very cold and very drunk.

I was too drunk to write at my desk. I was nervous, too. All night long my inner voice urged me to run out of my room, run down the hall and go pounding on Jeremy's door. What for? What was my hurry? All was decided, was it not? In the end I did nothing but spend the night pacing up and down in my room,

I had a mid-morning breakfast at the club. I took coffee, toast and juice and then went down to the main lounge to read the Times. I hoped to run into Jeremy there but was disappointed. When I finished the paper I looked at my watch. It was only ten thirty five.

I went down to the lobby and struck up a conversation with Timothy, who happened to be on duty that morning. Timothy was growing into his job. His eyes no longer stared vacantly; he was beginning to learn a few key Manhattan addresses. I am sure he would turn out to be a valued employee over the years.

"How's it going, Timothy?"

The young man straightened up and nodded formally.

"Morning, Mr. Lattimore. Things are going well, sir. Oh! Miss Knoffer left her job, sir. Did you hear that, sir?"

"I'm afraid I did."

"She was really pretty."

"Yes, she was."

Our conversation fizzled out. I was going to ask Timothy where I could put in a job application for this place but I did not; such a thing would never work out for me and I knew it. I looked at my watch. It was not quite a quarter to eleven.

I went back to my room and paced about again. I still liked room 813, yet perhaps it was time for a change of rooms once again. Down at the desk were employees I knew, but not well. Now that Judy was gone I would have to cultivate someone else's attention to help me with my eccentricities. I resumed pacing until, and finally, it was time.

I left my room and walked down the hall to room 806. I knocked on the door. There was no answer and the door sagged inward. Obviously he had left it open for me. I knocked again. There was no answer.

"Jeremy?"

I shoved the door inward and peered inside. He was not in the room but the water was running in the bath. I let myself in and took a seat at his desk. There was an open notebook on the desk but I did not look at it. I looked around, instead. The man's bags were not packed; obviously he was not leaving quite as soon as I expected. The bed was unmade. Where was Margo, the woman who cleaned the rooms on our floor when Adele was not there? Margo was a vivacious young woman from Sweden, a buxom girl and as energetic as any human being could be. I liked her and I just knew we would get along fine if it turned out that she was to be Adele's permanent replacement. I knew that Margo liked me, too. Already she was bringing me little cakes that she baked herself.

I waited and waited. Neither Jeremy nor Margo appeared. The water kept on running. Finally I shouted:

"Jeremy?"

If he was in the shower he couldn't hear me. I knocked on the bathroom door but still got no answer. Finally I opened that door and stuck my head inside. The room was filled with steam and I could not see anything even though the lights were turned on. Water was spilling over the edge of the tub onto the tiled floor.

"Say, Jeremy!"

I waited a moment until the steam cleared and then stepped all the way into the bathroom. I drew back the curtain about the tub and stared. Jeremy's eyes stared back at me. The entire right side of his head was blown apart and the fat revolver was still clutched in his right hand, which was lying draped over the rim of the tub. The flowing water was slightly discolored, looking like diluted ketchup. I turned off the faucets and grinned softly.

"Well, Jeremy," I said to the body, in a whisper. "Is this what the inner life gets you?"

I realized that the gun must have gone off with a roar but the singing of the pipes was no loud that, obviously, no one heard the shot. I backed out of the bathroom but not before turning on the faucets again. I did not want to be in this room when Margo finally entered it. Not that I would have any explaining to do. It was just that it would be better if the maid reported this tragedy downstairs.

I moved swiftly through the room towards the outer door. As I was passing the desk I had been sitting at I happened to glance sideways and Jeremy's open notebook caught my attention. I paused to look at what was written on the page.

I don't know why I hadn't looked at it before. No matter, I could read it now. It was not a suicide note; at least I do not think it was. It was a one-liner and to this day I wonder whether it Jeffery meant it for me or for him. It said:

"Winner takes all."

I went out of the room leaving the door ajar. I returned to my own room without being seen.

***

That was twelve years ago. Margo, who did come on duty late and did discover the body, called the desk as soon as she could control her screaming. After a few minutes I ran out of my room to see what all the noise was about. Margo was babbling to all the club personnel and finally turned to me. She found me a sympathetic listener. We became lovers two months later.

"Winner takes all."

After the body was removed I sat in my room for hours on end wondering what to do. I wanted to do the right thing. I knew that Jeremy Lighter left no family. He was like me in that regard. So I could not turn the ticket over to his wife, or to his mother or to his sister. There was no one. I did think of going over to Grand Central Station, to that newspaper stand, to tell the clerk on duty that a fellow I knew bought a quick pick and asked me to check his numbers for him and that I did check his numbers and found out that he was a winner. I found out that he was worth thirty seven million dollars. I would say to the clerk:

"The winner killed himself and left no family. I don't know to whom this money belongs. Maybe I ought to turn it over to the State. Here. You are in charge of these things. You do it."

Right.

I held onto the ticket until there were just a few hours left in the one year since it was purchased. Then I cashed it. It would have been a waste to let it run out. I continued to live as I had been living, the rest you know.

Now that I am living in it I know that great-grandfather's suite is just the right size for me. I am not getting any younger; I feel a need for the extra space.

I have recently cultivated the friendship and attention of a new assistant manager as well. Her name is Susan. She does not bother me with talk of marriage or of raised ranch houses; at the moment she thinks it wildly romantic to slip into my bed a couple of times a week after she gets off duty and once Margo has left the building.

One other thing: I have found a publisher for my midnight scribbling. My insightful guide for the gentleman of leisure will not be a best seller. I take great comfort in that.